I0451329

Foundling

Curse of the Hybrids

Book 2

LISA LAGALY

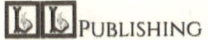PUBLISHING

Published in the United States of America

First Printing, 2025

ISBN
ebook: 978-1-966455-06-6
print: 978-1-966455-07-3

LL Publishing
Lisal.author@gmail.com

Dedicated

To my middle child.
Musician, mathlete, runner, student.
Lover of random facts and (gasp) non-fiction books.

```
      0 1            1 0
    1 0 0 1        0 0 1 0
  0 0 0 0 0      1 1 0 1 1
  0 0 0 1 1 0 1 1 1 1 0
  1 1 1 0 1 1 0 0 1 1 0
  0 1 0 1 0 0 1 0 0 0 0
    0 0 1 1 1 1 0 0 1
      0 1 1 0 1 1 1
        1 0 1 1 1
          0 1 0
            1
```

A Cautionary Note

This book is free of in-depth descriptions of romantic escapades and ridiculous amounts of cussing, but other things that people might find disturbing do happen such as what happened to Honey's parents. In this story, one of the characters was spelled which makes him depressed and suicidal.

1

Honey

Smoke was pouring from her house. She knew you were not supposed to enter a burning house but she ran through the backdoor and into the kitchen anyway.

"Mom, where are you?"

The small kitchen was empty. She hurried into the smoke-filled living room and frantically spun around, searching.

"Mom?"

There. On the floor just outside the bedroom.

"Mom! Dad? No! Please don't be dead. Wake up. Look at me."

"Honey, wake up. It's just a dream."

"Mom, I'm here. Please look at me."

Her leg shook.

"Honey, you're having another nightmare. Wake up."

Honey blinked. The flames and smoke and smell of burnt flesh abruptly vanished to be replaced by cool darkness that smelled of books and magic and old dorm.

"You all right?"

Her roommate's pale face was a dim moon at the foot of their shared bunk bed.

"Yeah. Thanks Blaze. Sorry I woke you again."

How many times was that now? Blaze had been extremely patient and understanding. Honey had really lucked out on roommates.

"You didn't. I just got back. It's Halloween you know, or it was."

Right. She'd forgotten about Halloween what with getting stabbed and capturing the witch who'd caused her to be stabbed and the celebration last night when Brayton's charges were dropped.

"You want to talk about it?" Blaze asked.

Honey shook her head. "There's nothing to talk about. It's the same dream every time, but thanks for asking."

"Your parents?"

Honey nodded.

Blaze squeezed her ankle. "That's what roommates are for. You know, I bet Gloria has some herbs that will help."

"She gave me some of her calming tea. If I can't get back to sleep, I'll take it."

"Good. I'm going to take a shower."

Honey rolled over, wiping her tears off on the pillow while she turned. She didn't need calming tea. She needed her parents back.

She didn't think she'd be able to fall asleep again, but suddenly her alarm was going off and she was yanked from another dream. It wasn't of the fire this time though. No, this one featured the thin, tortured face of the young man she'd met in the bar.

It wasn't the first time she'd dreamed of Zavier. Since speaking with him at the bar last Friday, she couldn't get him out of her mind. He was a drunk and an attempted murderer, but he didn't want to be. He'd only drank to get rid of the headaches caused by the cursed drink. He'd felt so guilty about what he'd been forced to do and what he'd become, he'd nearly succeeded in ending his own life.

Had nearly dying reset his brain and destroyed the curse? Was he still in pain? Brayton had thrown up from the pain. Was Zavier's just as bad? If she could just see him alone, she might be able to help him the way she'd helped Brayton.

By Friday, she couldn't stand wondering how he was anymore. She called the number for the wolf doctor's clinic/hospital. The receptionist told her Zavier was still there, but she wouldn't tell Honey his condition. Honey left a message for the doctor and went to her next class. Dr. Ziga called while she was in class and left a message to say the witch healer had seen him, but that was all he said.

She didn't know why she was so concerned for Zavier. The first time they'd met he'd made her very uncomfortable, and the second time was right after he'd hurt a lot of people, but something kept urging her to help.

After her last class, she dropped her bag off in her room and set off for the two mile walk to the clinic in the rain.

She was half-afraid the wolves at the clinic wouldn't let her see him since she wasn't family, but the receptionist pointed to the hall when she asked for his room number. He was in the room next to the one she'd been in after she was stabbed.

Zavier didn't look any better than the last time she'd seen him, which was saying something because he'd looked awful then. He didn't smell as bad, but his skin was pale and waxy, his dark longish hair was lank and oily-looking, and he was so thin she could nearly see his skull through his skin. He didn't respond at all when she called his name and shook his arm. If not for the quite beep of the heart monitor, he could easily pass for dead.

He was a wolf. It had been five days since he'd attempted to hang himself. He should be better. The curse must still be working. There was only one way she knew of to find out.

Only her four best friends, 'the guys' she liked to call them, knew the truth about her. She was both witch and wolf – a wolch. She wasn't supposed to exist. She'd only learned recently that it was illegal for her to even be alive.

Liam would tell her she was being foolish to risk getting caught, but the young man in front of her didn't deserve what had happened to him. If he was still under the influence of the curse, she might be the only one who could help, which meant she had to help. Well, not had to. She had a choice, but powers were a gift from God and meant to be used to help others. Mom had believed it and so did she.

After shutting the door and cracking the window, she dragged a chair to the side of his bed, close enough that she could touch Zavier's head. She didn't really want to touch his greasy scalp, but the closer she got, the easier it would be and the less magic she had to use.

She only meant to look but his head was a mess. It felt like every single molecule was going the wrong way. It took her several minutes of searching to find one that felt right. From there, she started turning the molecules nearby until they felt right too.

It was a stupid thing to do.

She was so lost in Zavier's head that she didn't hear the door open. She didn't have time to clear the air of magic. She didn't realize anyone else was there until a heavy hand landed on her shoulder and a male voice said, "Stop whatever you're doing and let's talk."

Reluctantly, she released her hold on a molecule she'd half-convinced to turn and returned her focus to the rest of the world. "Dr. Ziga, I can explain."

"I certainly hope so."

She didn't want to remove her fingers from Zavier's head. The wrongness of the molecules begged to be fixed, but she was also beginning to feel the effects of using so much magic. She dropped her hands into her lap and turned to the doctor.

Why did he let the hair on his ears grow so long? It grew more from the edge of his ears than the center and blended with the curly graying hair on the top of his head, but you could tell.

"Admiring my ear hair?" he asked.

"Umm."

"It's more common among people from India and some consider it a sign of luck and prosperity."

"Are you from India?"

"No, but my grandfather was. Now explain, please, what you were doing to my patient."

She glanced at Zavier, so deathly pale on the bed. If she had to guess, she'd say he was only in his twenties, but he looked older with his skin so sickly pale and nearly translucent. It pained her to see someone who should have been in his prime looking that way.

She couldn't think how to explain away the smell of magic in the room, so she told Dr. Ziga the truth, well, part of it. "You were wrong about my brain."

"Was I?" Dr. Ziga didn't sound at all surprised. She turned toward him again so she could watch his face.

"That part that doesn't do telepathy doesn't make me smarter. It gives me magic."

He raised an eyebrow. It was as impressively furry as his ears. "You're a wolf with magic?"

"All wolves have magic. Mine is just different." This wasn't something she had concluded. She and her mom had often discussed how wolves and witches had come into being. Mom's theory was that they shared a common ancestor, but at some point one or more of those ancestors capable of shape-shifting had been isolated and formed the first colony of wolves. Now Honey wondered if maybe it hadn't been two witches – one shape-shifter and one with telepathy.

"Uh-huh, and what does your magic do? Specifically, what were you doing to my patient?"

"I can see and manipulate molecules. I just wanted to look into his head and see what was wrong." Her mother had never heard of magic like hers, but perhaps it was due to the way Honey explained it. After an enlightening talk with her friends about what grade school was like, she was pretty sure most witches didn't have the chemistry lessons to refer to that she did at the age of five.

If her explanation seemed odd to Dr. Ziga, he gave no sign. "Did you find anything?"

Honey reached up and covered Zavier's cold, limp hand. She was pretty sure Zavior couldn't hear her, but what she was about to say was scary.

10

"Yeah. Almost every molecule in his brain is going the wrong direction."

"What do you mean? Do you mean they're flowing the wrong way in the blood?"

"No. Molecules are always wiggling and spinning and bouncing. His are just…spinning the wrong direction." Spinning wasn't really the right term, but it was the best explanation she could give.

"How can you tell? Isn't it random?"

She shrugged. "I just can."

"Can you make them spin the right way?"

"Yes."

"Is that why it smells so strongly of magic in here?"

"Yes."

"Did you get them all spinning the same way?"

"No. That will take a while."

"How long?"

She pictured the mess that was Zavior's head. She'd worked for nearly an hour according to the clock on the wall, but barely accomplished anything. It was discouraging. "Nine to ten hours at least. I had trouble finding molecules that weren't going the wrong way."

"Have you done this before?"

"Yes. It's how I fixed Brayton's headaches."

"Ah," Dr. Ziga said, nodding, "so it wasn't massage. I was feeling quite put-out that you could help him just by rubbing his temples after I tried everything I could think of."

"Sorry?"

He chuckled. "I'm just glad he's better. Despite all the medical advances made over the thousands of years humans and wolves and witches have existed, sometimes

11

we doctors still can't identify the underlying cause of an illness. We can only treat the symptoms. Are you planning to stay all night and work on his head?"

"I can't. It takes too much effort. The longest I've made it is two hours, and then I fell asleep under a bush."

Dr. Ziga nodded. "We don't want that. This will be a long-term treatment then. Can you handle an hour each day?"

"Maybe. What did Gene, the Enforcer healer say? Is there any chance she can help?"

"She confirmed he was under the influence of a spell. The Enforcers were able to obtain the recipe from the creator of the spell, but part of the magic is unique to the creator. Gene didn't know how to break the spell other than to let it wear off. I also contacted the witch council, but I haven't heard back from them yet."

Honey rubbed her fingers against the back of Zavier's hand. His skin was thin and cool where she hadn't been touching him. "It would be better if they could heal him. Their ways would probably be faster and I really don't know what I'm doing. I'm just going by instinct."

"Sometimes instinctual magic is the best kind. I'll call them again after we're done here. They probably won't answer though. Witches tend to take Friday afternoons off. Can you come in tomorrow? The faster we can heal him, the better. His vitals don't look good and the witches aren't known for their speed, especially when it comes to helping wolves."

Liam's harsh words sounded in her head. "What if I'm doing it wrong? What if I hurt him?"

Dr. Ziga squeezed her shoulder. "He's already hurt. Doctors don't always know exactly how to help someone.

12

We rely on our experience and make our best guess. My experience is telling me to let you continue. I'm not sure he'll survive otherwise."

She nodded. Not doing anything was more deadly than doing something. Besides, Brayton seemed fine now. He'd survived her molecule manipulation, as Luca called it.

"I can come in, but I don't want anyone to know what I can do."

The doctor nodded. "We can keep the door shut and run the exhaust fan. If anyone asks, you can tell them you're shadowing me for a couple of weeks. You can do that too while you're here, so it's true. Pre-med students do it all the time."

"I'm not pre-med."

"You're young. Plenty of time to look into it. Wolf doctors are always in demand and alphas tend to overlook oddities when the members are otherwise beneficial to the pack."

"You mean my lack of telepathy?"

He nodded, but he was smiling too.

"Are you considered odd?"

Dr. Ziga laughed. "Did the ear hair not give you a clue? Now, what time can you come by tomorrow?"

Tomorrow was Saturday. She had a paper to write, an exam to study for, and at some point, a costume to find since Charlize had decided to hold a Halloween party after all since all charges against Brayton, the future alpha of their pack, had been dropped. She was calling it a costume party now since Halloween was over.

"Noon?" That would give her time to rest before she and the boys went shopping.

He pulled a phone out of his pocket and swiped across the screen. "Give me your number. I'll text you if the witches are coming."

"What about visitors?"

"We'll deal with them if we have to. He hasn't received any since last Sunday. I heard he was thrown out of the pack before it was determined the witch was responsible. Generally, that means his family can't visit him."

"Won't the pack take him back in since he's innocent?"

"You would think."

She patted Zavier's hand. She couldn't imagine...no she could. She could imagine Alpha Brandon throwing someone out of the pack if they tried to murder a bunch of people, but would he really forbid his family from seeing him? Zavier was a drunk, but from what he'd told her that night at the club after he'd been arrested, he'd only drank the special Blue Juice the waitress had served him to get rid of his headaches.

Luna Lynn had mentioned he had an engineering degree and a girlfriend. She wondered what had happened to the girlfriend.

2

Honey

Saturday worked out perfectly. She got her homework out of the way, worked on Zavier for forty-five minutes, and had plenty of time for a nap before costume shopping with the guys. Walter wanted to go as Power Rangers. Thankfully, Luca and Nathan overrode that idea and they all decided to go as superheroes. She got off easy. Thanks to Luna Lynn, she already had clothes appropriate to dress as the Black Widow. She just needed some thigh holsters and fake guns. She also got some temporary red hair dye. There was no way she was going to ask Sabine to magically change her hair. Sabine was still grumping about all the requests people had made for her help on Halloween.

The party was in the fancy new girls' dorm – the sister dorm to the one where the boys stayed. There were a few others who dressed as superheroes, but none of them looked as good as her group. Blond Nathan was Captain America. Tan Luca was Hawkeye. Tall, slim Walter was Dr. Strange and cocoa-skinned Liam was the Black

Panther. He made a great Black Panther. Charlize couldn't keep her eyes off him. Their group got first place in the group costume category. There was a lot more to do – Charlize was an excellent organizer, but Honey was so tired she left right after the awards.

Sunday, she went to see Zavier again after church. She lost track of time and worked on him for over an hour and a half. She was so tired, Dr. Ziga insisted on driving her to the dorms, then ordered her to take the next day off. She didn't want to. She wanted to get the job over with and she was worried about Zavier. He looked worse every time she saw him even though Dr. Ziga ensured her that he wasn't.

"Hey, Honey!"

If she'd just been a few steps closer to the door of her dorm, she could have pretended not to hear, but Brayton inserted himself between her and safety and grinned. She hadn't spoken with him much since Halloween when he'd not only hugged her but kissed her on the forehead to thank her for helping get his charges dropped. Prior to that she couldn't remember him ever grinning at her. It made him look deceptively friendly.

"I've come up with some simple signals we can try on our next run."

"Okay."

She was so tired, all she wanted to do was crawl in bed and hibernate. She yawned and moved to go around him, but he moved with her.

"Here. I drew them out so you can memorize them."

He waved a piece of paper in her face. Why did he want to discuss this now? The next full moon wasn't until after Thanksgiving. She took the paper and glanced at it to

16

be polite. It was covered front to back in squares with little sketches. Looking at it made her want to bury herself in her bed and sleep a few weeks.

"Thank you." She said because it was the polite thing to do, or perhaps she just thought it. Brayton shook her shoulder and she realized she'd dozed off where she was standing.

"Honey, are you listening to me?"

She forced her eyes open to look at him. He wasn't smiling any more. "What did you say?"

"What's wrong with you?"

"Tired." She shut her eyes again. Was it possible for her to sleep standing? That might be useful.

Brayton shook her awake again. "Honey, wake up. Who dropped you off? I didn't recognize the car."

"Dr. Ziga."

"You went to see Dr. Ziga?" She'd already closed her eyes again, so she couldn't see his expression, but his voice held a note of concern.

She nodded.

"Is something wrong?"

"No." She felt and smelled him move closer. He had the nicest body spray or soap or whatever boys used.

"Do you have a headache?"

He was close enough that she felt his breath on her cheek, but she didn't open her eyes. She was really tempted to lean on his shoulder so she wouldn't have to hold her head up anymore. "No. Tired."

He felt her forehead. That was unexpected. She opened her eyes to his frown.

"Why are you so tired? Did you go out somewhere after you left the party?"

17

"No." She yawned again. Something in her jaw popped.

"Did you hang out with your friends?"

She nodded. She had, but not that late. She was in bed by eleven.

"Honey! Wake up!"

Her eyes had somehow closed again.

"You're falling asleep on your feet, literally." Brayton stepped aside and pushed her toward the door. "Get to bed."

"I was trying to," she mumbled, maybe. She stumbled up the stairs and climbed into bed. She didn't wake up until 5:15 am Monday morning but she made it to her 5:30 WOLF class with one minute to spare and she did feel a lot better.

She visited Zavier again on Tuesday and every day the rest of the week. She made sure to do her homework and eat supper first and that Dr. Ziga pulled her away after forty-five minutes. He drove her home after every session and she went straight to bed. It was still really tough getting up at 5:10 am in the morning to go to WOLF training on Friday. Worse, despite all her efforts, Zavier didn't look like he was improving.

Luca, Nathan, and Walter were waiting for her when she stumbled out of the dorm on Friday morning even though they only had five minutes to get to class.

"You guys should have gone ahead without me."

Luca threw his arm over her shoulders. "We wouldn't leave you behind. Besides, Liam went ahead to tell Captain Young we're coming. You ready to run? We can get there in time if we go fast."

"Sure."

"You look tired," Walter said, studying her under the streetlight. "How much longer do you think it will take?"

They all knew what she was doing. Liam thought it was stupid and dangerous, but the rest of them were supportive.

"I'm over half-done. If I get a good sleep tonight and tomorrow, I might be able to finish this weekend."

"Good. We miss you," Luca said. "There's no one who can beat Walter at Trivial Pursuit like you can."

"You guys don't play that often."

"Only because you haven't been there."

She rolled her eyes and started running. She wasn't as fast as she normally was. Using magic every day was wearing her down. She was hoping her magic would get stronger and last longer with use, like a muscle, but she wasn't feeling it yet.

They made it onto the field just as class officially began. It had been so warm lately she'd assumed it would be warm again. Wrong. It was freezing outside, literally. It was so cold she volunteered to practice in wolf form for once. She jogged the warm-up laps in her human form to give everyone else time to change, ran into the girls' changing tent, then right back out. Cici was still inside. Honey gave up on the tent and ran for the port-a-potty.

Walter was waiting for her when she opened the door. He pretended to take some clothes from her but really it was just his coat rolled into a bundle. Cici must have followed her again. If it was just a matter of undressing instead of making her clothes vanish when she transformed, something no other wolf could do, she might consider transforming in the tent in front of everyone.

19

However, her instantaneous transformations on top of her inability to speak telepathically in wolf form – something she'd only learned wolves could do in the last month – were also odd. How that would lead people to guess she was half witch, she didn't know, but her father had warned her not to let other wolves see her transform, and other than the guys, no one else had.

She made it through training without screwing up too badly. Not being able to speak telepathically to the wolves she was training with was challenging, but everyone in the pack now knew that she couldn't hear them, so they didn't expect her to coordinate her movements perfectly with theirs. She must have been a little off though because Captain Young asked her if she was feeling okay.

After training, she bypassed the tent and Cici and went directly to the port-a-potty. It smelled strongly of disinfectant, which was generally better than the alternative, but it was still tough on her wolf nose. Anxious to get away from the smell as soon as she could, she pictured her human form even as she pulled the door shut with her paw. The tingle of the change rippled across her skin, but her eye-level view of the toilet seat didn't change. She tried again. This time there wasn't even a tingle. Her chest clenched. Her second greatest fear had come true. She was stuck.

Walter was standing right where she'd left him outside the potty when she finally gave up and pushed open the door. "Honey, why didn't you change?"

She whined and ran toward the edge of the parking lot by the field where fine dirt separated the pavement from the grass, then used her nail to write, "*I'm stuck*" in the dirt.

"Stuck? How's that possible?"

20

She shrugged.

He waved the other guys over and explained the situation.

"Are you sure?" Luca asked. "I've never heard of that happening. Try again. No one's paying any attention."

She looked past his legs. He was right. Most people were already walking away from the field and toward the dorms. She tried. There was a tingle again but no change. She shook her head.

"She did look tired earlier and she clearly wasn't herself during practice. Maybe she's just too weak to change," Nathan said.

"Or maybe you've used up your magic," Liam said. "I told you it was dangerous to help that guy."

She growled.

"He might be right," Walter said, "but it shouldn't be permanent. If a wolf transforms several times in a row, they will eventually get too tired and be stuck in whatever form they ended in for a while. I bet magic takes a toll on you just like transformation."

She whined again and wrote "*Math test*" in the dirt.

Walter shook his head. "That's not going to happen. You're going to be stuck as a wolf for several hours at least."

That's what he thought.

"The best thing for you to do is rest. You can stay in our rooms and veg on the couch. We'll bring you food."

She shook her head. They weren't allowed to run around campus in their wolf forms. He knew that.

Luca squatted down and started running his hand over her head. In human form it would have been weird, but as a wolf she liked it. "You can't stay here. It's supposed to

21

snow later. The humans won't know. You're so small, you can pass for a dog."

She made a sound of displeasure.

"A very pretty dog," he amended.

She licked his cheek, knowing how gross it was.

"Ew, really Honey?"

"He's not wiping it off," Nathan noted.

"I think he liked it," Walter said. "Was that your first kiss, Luca?"

"It's more than you've got," Luca said defiantly.

Honey rolled her eyes and headed toward the dorms, leaving them standing there in a circle sharing insults like the silly boys they were. Her calculus teacher was a wolf. If she could figure out how to write with her nail, maybe she could still take the test, not in class where everyone could see her, of course, but maybe behind his desk. She needed food first though.

The boys caught up with her a few seconds later as she'd known they would.

"Whoa, Miss Smith, where are you going?" Captain Young called just as they passed the bleachers.

"She's stuck," Luca said.

"We think she wore herself out," Nathan added.

"Stuck? Are you sure? You know you can't go on campus like that, right?"

"Yes, we're sure and we know," Walter said, "but she has to eat."

"True, but you need to go to the doctor if you're truly stuck. This could be serious."

"We'll take her to Dr. Ziga," Nathan declared.

"Bring your car here and pick her up. Did you guys get her clothes?"

22

"She's good," Walter said, patting Luca's backpack. Luca always stuffed his clothes in a bag instead of folding them and leaving them in a nice pile like everyone else. She didn't see him do it, obviously. She knew because of how much the other guys teased him, and because he always carried a bag to training.

Walter drove. The guys couldn't stay long. They had a test in their first class at 9 am. They left her by the front desk with a bag of breakfast goodies Luca had snatched from the cafeteria. Dr. Ziga's receptionist didn't appear worried at all about Honey's predicament, which made her feel a little better.

Dr. Ziga exited an exam room about ten minutes after Honey arrived, followed by a very pregnant woman. The woman was so large and waddling so badly, it looked like she was going to pop out some kids any moment. The tall, thin man sitting on the chair across the reception area from Honey hopped up and rushed to her side. Dr. Ziga shook his head at the man. "Not yet, but soon."

"Can't she stay?" the man asked. He reeked of worry.

The woman slapped his arm. "No! I'm fine. I told you I was fine. It was just my body getting ready."

"It's good to be cautious," Dr. Ziga said diplomatically. "Especially in your case. I want you to come in the moment you feel like it might be time, even if it isn't. It doesn't hurt to keep an eye on things."

Dr. Ziga watched while the man escorted his wife to a beat-up truck in the small parking lot behind the house. Despite her bulk, the woman refused her husband's help and hoisted herself up into the cab. Dr. Ziga shook his head, then turned to Honey.

23

"Triplets, yet she's determined nothing is going to slow her down and they are going to be born when she's ready and not a moment sooner. She'll be back tomorrow at the latest. And you," he shook his finger at Honey. "I knew I should have told you to take a break yesterday. Come on. I've got something I want to show you. Bring your food."

They may have just been pastries from the school cafeteria, but she was hungry and they were right under her nose. By the time she got to Zavier's room, the top of the bag was dripping with her saliva. Gross. Dr. Ziga took it from her and nonchalantly ripped the top off the bag, then pulled out a cheesy bacon scone.

"Mind if I take this?"

There was a huge muffin and a croissant too, so she truly didn't.

"Watch this."

He leaned over the body on the bed. Honey put her paws on the edge of the bed to see what he was doing. He waved the pastry under Zavier's nose.

"Zavier, it's time to wake up. I've got a treat for you. That's it. Use those wolf senses of yours. You haven't had a solid bite to eat in two weeks. Aren't you hungry?"

Zavier's nose twitched. That was the first voluntary movement Honey had seen him make since she started treating him.

"That's right. It's bacon." Dr. Ziga broke off a piece and waved it under Zavier's nose. "Smell that. Fresh from the oven."

Honey's mouth started salivating again. Why had she agreed to share? She might have whined.

"Here Honey." Dr. Ziga tossed the piece to her and she snapped it out of the air. "You better wake up if you want some Zavier. Honey here is pretty hungry. She might eat it all herself."

Zavier's lips trembled and he growled.

Dr. Ziga tore off another piece and waved it under Zavier's nose. "Wake up if you want it. No? Okay, I'll eat it then." He popped the second piece into his mouth. Zavier snapped his teeth.

"He's close," Dr. Ziga said. "Last night he only wiggled his nose, and yes, I do this all the time. I've found it's the most accurate way to see if a wolf is nearing consciousness."

Zavier's hand abruptly moved and wrapped around Dr. Ziga's arm. Dr. Ziga tore off a piece of scone and put it against Zavier's lips. "If you're awake enough to move, you're awake enough to eat. Open up."

Zavier did! He ate three bites and then opened his eyes too.

"Ha. There you are. Welcome back to the world."

Zavier blinked at him, then started looking around the room, looking slightly puzzled. He didn't say a word until his eyes fell on Honey.

"Mom?"

"No. She is most definitely not your mom. This is Honey."

"Honey?"

"Yes. She's been helping you. How's your head?"

Zavier winced and rubbed his forehead. "It hurts."

"Yes, you did quite a number on yourself. Here, finish the scone. I'll pour you some water to wash it down. Honey, you should eat too."

She dropped back down on the floor and stuck her nose in the bag and quickly devoured the contents. She then did her best to slurp up some water from the plastic cup Dr. Ziga offered her without splashing it all over the floor.

"Why is she in wolf form?" Zavier asked, peering down at her.

"She's stuck," Dr. Ziga said, "although hopefully not for long. Do you remember what happened?"

"I killed some people."

"No. You didn't kill them. They're fine."

"Are you sure? There was blood everywhere … and screaming. So much blood."

"I'm sure."

"I…what happened afterward? I don't remember."

"Honey and her friends helped capture the witch who put a spell on you. A couple of days later all charges were dropped. Unfortunately, the spell still lingers. It made you depressed and suicidal. You attempted to kill yourself and have been unconscious ever since."

Zavier lifted his hand to rub the center of his forehead. "How long?"

"Almost two weeks. Today is a Friday."

"I was banished, wasn't I?"

"You remember?"

"No. I can't feel the pack bond anymore. Did Alpha Meyer forbid my family from visiting me too?"

"I'm afraid so," Dr. Ziga said gently.

From her viewpoint on the floor, Honey saw a tear slip out from under the hand Zavier was holding over his eyes. She wanted to hold his hand and tell him everything would be okay, but she couldn't, so she jumped up in the chair next to the bed and laid her head on his chest. After a moment, his other hand started running down her fur.

"It wasn't your fault Zavier," Dr. Ziga said.

Zavier's chest started shaking under her chin.

"Keep an eye on him Honey."

Zavier's quiet sobs hurt her heart. She wanted to get closer and hug him, but there was no room on the hospital bed for a wolf, so she stayed where she was while his fingers petted and gripped and tangled in her fur. It wasn't hard enough to hurt. After a while, the shaking of his chest calmed. She thought he'd gone back to sleep until he started talking.

"He's wrong you know. It was my fault."

She wanted to deny it but the best she could do was make a little moaning sound. His fingers twisted in the fur on her head.

"After Katie broke up with me, I started drinking because it helped me forget for a while. I had dreams, you know, plans. We'd find a little house with a yard, have a few kids. I'd make my famous pancakes on Sunday." He sniffed. "I knew drinking was only a temporary fix, but I thought it would make it easier. It didn't. It just made me numb for a while. Without her life is – it's like a black and white movie."

She wanted to ask him why they'd broke up but had to settle for patting him with her paw.

"And now everything is messed up." He sobbed a few more times. "I've lost my job. My family and my pack think I'm nothing but a useless drunk, and now I'm a rogue. What's the point? You should have let me end it."

Despair was oozing off of him like mud off a swamp monster. She couldn't smell magic, but she was certain at least part of it was the curse talking.

He lifted his hand away from her head and pushed on her shoulder. "You should go. Don't waste your time with me."

She lifted her head enough to look at him properly, but she refused to move any further. He didn't have enough strength after lying in bed for two weeks to come close to budging her.

"I said go!" He flung his hand toward the door like she was a dog to command.

She stretched up and nuzzled his chin with her nose. He smelled like hospital and the soap the nurses used to give him a sponge bath.

"What do I have to do to get you to leave?"

She licked his jaw. It wasn't a big lick, just enough to let him know she wasn't leaving.

He touched the spot and looked down at her, puzzled. "Why did you do that? Do I know you? Did mom send you?"

She wished she could say yes, but she shook her head.

"Your eyes look familiar though. Have we met before?"

Finally, she could nod.

He sniffed the air. "You don't smell like my pack." He frowned. "You smell like Little *and* Mooney. How is that possible?"

She tilted her head and raised an eyebrow.

"Let's try yes or no questions. Are you a nurse? No. A doctor? No." He studied her for a moment. "Did we meet at the club?"

She nodded.

"Did I hit on you?"

How to answer that one? He had the first time, but not the second. She nodded, then shook her head.

"I don't know what that means. Were you there the night I, I went mad?"

She nodded.

"Why are you here then? You saw what I did?"

She nodded.

"I should be dead."

She shook her head.

"Wait, are you an Enforcer? Are you here to guard me? No? I don't understand. Tell me who you are!"

He yelled the last bit.

She wished she could, but it had only been an hour since she tried to transform and she knew that wasn't long enough. She whined and put her head back on his chest.

After a moment, he put his hand back down on her head. "Sorry. My head feels like someone is pounding on it with a sledgehammer. The doctor said you were stuck, didn't he?"

She nodded.

"How did that happen?"

She sighed.

"Right. Yes or no. Did the witch curse you too? No." He rubbed his forehead with his other hand. "I don't suppose you could do something for my head, like get the doctor?"

Would it be safe to leave him? Dr. Ziga had said to keep an eye on him. Even if Dr. Ziga could help him, it would only be temporary until she could fix it. He was rubbing the front of his head. Maybe it was only a few molecules that were causing the problem.

"Why are you looking at me like that?" He closed his eyes and rubbed his head again. "Ugh. This is worse than before."

Looking wouldn't cost her much power but Zavier would smell the magic. He was going to smell it eventually though, since she still had hours of work to do on his head. Dr. Ziga seemed to think it was perfectly normal for her to have a different kind of magic then all other wolves. Well, not normal but understandable since she lacked telepathy. Hopefully Zavier would feel the same way.

It would be weird to lean over him in wolf form and touch her paws to his temples, so she looked into his head from where she was. There were pockets of molecules all over his brain that still needed tending. She focused on his forehead though since that was where he was rubbing. The molecules there, or whatever they were, did look angrier than some of the others. She didn't want to be stuck as a wolf all day, but she figured fixing a few molecules wouldn't hurt anything. She focused on the ones moving the fastest.

"Do you smell that? It smells like magic."

She ignored him. The biggest molecule was being extremely stubborn.

"Is that you? Ah. Ow. What are you doing? I can feel you in my head. Oh. That...feels better. Are you healing me? Are you a healer? How is that possible? I don't understand."

She didn't try to answer him. Her magic was there, but it was sluggish. She could handle a few spots though. She did as many as she could, then stopped fighting the darkness and let sleep take her.

3

Honey

Bacon. She smelled bacon and hamburger and cheddar cheese and somewhere, salty, greasy, slightly burned French fries.

"There she is."

She looked up from the burger to Dr. Ziga towering over her.

"Have a nice nap?"

She put her paws out in front of her and stretched. She was on a bed, but there wasn't much room. Zavier was taking up most of it. She was near his legs. How had she gotten into Zavier's bed? He smiled down at her from where he was propped up at the head of the bed and popped a fry into his mouth.

Dr. Ziga put the burger on a plate in front of her. "Eat, then we'll see how you feel. You slept for a solid nine hours. That should be enough to recharge you unless you completely drained your battery earlier." He gave her a stern look. "You can't help your patients properly if you're worn out yourself."

Did she hurt Zavier? she swung her head around to inspect him. He didn't look hurt.

"Eat Honey," Dr. Ziga commanded.

It's hard to eat a hamburger neatly when you're a wolf. She tried. The French fries were as delicious as they smelled, although a little cold. She sucked down the water Dr. Ziga offered her, then jumped down off the bed.

"Your clothes are in that bag your friends brought you. Go in the bathroom there and try to transform. I'll be right here in case anything goes wrong. I know you like your privacy, but if I don't hear from you in a few minutes, I'm coming in."

She grabbed Luca's bag with her teeth and carried it into the bathroom. She hoped he was right. She did feel better than she had this morning. She shut the door with her nose and dropped the bag on the floor. Taking a deep breath, she held it for a few seconds, then let her magic wash over her. She knew it had worked even before she opened her eyes and saw her human self in the mirror.

She let Dr. Ziga know she was human again by calling through the door, then took her time using the bathroom. It *had* been at least thirteen hours since the last time she'd had a chance.

If Dr. Ziga noticed the size of the bag hadn't changed, he didn't say anything.

"Honey?" Zavier asked.

"Yep. That's me." It was great to be able to talk again.

"Thank you for," he tapped his head.

"Is your headache better?"

"It's still there, but it's manageable. I'll be okay until you have a chance to rest more. Dr. Ziga explained everything."

33

She sat down in the chair beside him. Since his hand wasn't available, she touched his arm. "I haven't completely destroyed the curse yet. I think that's why you were feeling down earlier. Don't let it win."

He looked at her, then down to his lap. A single tear ran down his cheek. "Everything I said was true, though."

"So? You can find another job. I'm sure your family still loves you, and if your pack won't take you back, I know a pack that will."

"I doubt it."

She punched him. "The Mooney pack took me and look how messed up I am, although they don't know about the magic part yet, just the non-telepathy part. You'll keep that to yourself, I hope?"

"Yeah, but why?"

"You don't think it will cause problems?" she asked curiously. "Do you think other wolves will just accept that I have magic and everything will be fine?"

"You're a curse-breaker. I think wolves would be glad to finally have a way to defend themselves against the witches."

"I was able to break *one* curse. That's not actually what my magic does, it just happened to work this time."

"Have you tried it on another curse?"

"No."

"Maybe you should."

"If I run into another, maybe I will."

"Honey, if you're ready to go, there are five very impatient boys waiting out in the lobby," Dr. Ziga informed her.

"Five?" She and Zavier said at the same time.

"Yep." Dr. Ziga popped his 'P'. "You've got competition, Zavier."

She glared at Dr. Ziga. He had a strange sense of humor sometimes. "Stop that. Zavier, I'll tell you another secret, but keep it to yourself, okay?"

"What, are you gay?"

"No. I'm only fourteen. I haven't told my friends because they're all college students and I don't want to be treated any differently. I'm telling you because well," mentioning Katie and how she'd seen him looking for someone to replace her was probably the wrong thing to do. "I just thought you should know."

"You're fourteen? But Dr. Ziga said you were a freshman in college."

"I am."

He blinked at her. "Wow. I mean, I thought you looked young, but not that young."

"Um, thanks." she patted his arm. "I'll see you tomorrow, okay?"

He sighed. She didn't like the way he sounded, not with the curse still messing with his head. "How tired are you?"

"He slept almost as long as you did," Dr. Ziga said helpfully.

"Are you up for a game? We could play Scrabble or Trivial pursuit or something else. They have a lot of games at the front desk of my dorm."

"I'm not..."

"Movie it is then! I'll see if the guys want to join us. My mom and I used to have movie night every Friday. It will be fun. I'll get some popcorn and some drinks. What do you want? Oh, and brownies. I can get some from the cafeteria if they have them."

"I don't…"

"I'm not going to leave you here alone with that curse in your head."

"Sounds good," Dr. Ziga said, ignoring Zavier's pleading look. "I want a Dr. Pepper."

Who on Earth was the fifth guy she wondered while she walked down the hall. Had Greg come with the others? She stepped into the reception area. Luca, Nathan, Liam, and Walter were all sitting in a row, arguing about something as usual. She didn't see a fifth person. "Hey guys!"

Luca popped up first and nearly knocked her over with his hug. "Honey, you're not furry anymore!"

"Furry Honey. That's a great one," Nathan said, shaking his head. He pushed Luca away and pulled her into a hug next.

"Glad you're better," Walter said, pulling her away from Nathan and engulfing her in his long arms.

Liam didn't say anything. He just looked at her with his arms crossed and shook his head. She rolled her eyes and turned to the other three. "You guys want to do a movie night?"

"Sure!" Luca said. "What movie?"

"How about superheroes? Zavier is awake but the curse is still affecting him. I want something to keep him distracted until I can help him again."

"No. Not again," Liam said, stomping forward and pushing Luca out of the way so he could put his hands on

36

her shoulders. "You don't know what you're doing. You got stuck. What if you stayed that way permanently."

It was the first time he'd touched her in weeks. Instead of knocking his arms away like she would have in WOLF, she put her hands over his.

"Liam, he might die if I don't help him. He would have died."

"You don't know that."

"I do. How long did it take you to learn telepathy?"

"I didn't learn. I always knew how."

"Exactly. This is my telepathy."

"No, it's not. It's magic. You told me yourself you didn't know what you were doing."

"What's magic?"

Her heart jumped into her throat, but she tried to express only calm as she turned around. Liam's hands fell from her shoulders. "Brayton, what are you doing here?"

He shook his phone at her. "You didn't answer your phone. Mom was worried."

"I was sleeping."

"I heard. What did you do to wear yourself out so much? Are the classes too much for you?"

"No!"

"You guys been taking her to the clubs?"

"No, they haven't," Honey answered before her friends could. "I've been coming up here to help with Zavier."

"Is that why Dr. Ziga has been dropping you off?"

"Yes."

"How is he?"

She had no control over the smile that spread across her face. "He woke up! I was afraid he was getting worse,

37

but he finally woke this morning. The curse is still affecting him though, so we're going to have movie night here. I don't want him to be alone."

"*You* don't?"

"Dr. Ziga agrees." She had a sudden thought. "Brayton, his alpha kicked Zavier out before the Enforcers proved it wasn't his fault. Now that he's been shown to be innocent, will his alpha take him back? I think it would help if he could see his family."

She could tell Brayton was thinking from the appearance of the little line between his eyebrows. "It might not be that easy. Alpha Meyer is stubborn and Zavier has been having problems for a while."

"Could he at least see his family?" she asked.

"I'll see if Mom can do something. She's good at talking people into things."

"Thank you, Brayton."

4

Honey

"You all have fun last night?"

Honey stretched, careful not to whack the bed frame beside her again and opened her eyes. Dr. Ziga was standing at the door looking very amused at the unorganized mess of sleeping bags and blankets on the floor. When she and Walter and had gone back to the dorms to get supplies, he'd had the foresight to grab some sleeping gear too. She didn't have a sleeping bag so she'd brought the blankets off her bed.

"Yep," Luca said. "We even got pizza." He waved at the open, greasy box with one piece of pizza remaining in the middle of the floor.

"And how's our patient?"

"He fell asleep in the middle of our Iron-Man-athon," Honey said, sitting up and perusing the mess around her. Nathan had his sleeping bag up to his chin and was just starting to stir. Walter was sleeping hard flat on his back with his sleeping bag down to his waist and one leg poking out at the bottom through the zipper. Since she was closest to Zavier's bed, she pushed herself up to check on him. "Still breathing."

Zavier opened his eyes and frowned. "You're still here?"

"Yep."

"You mean the slumber party isn't over yet?"

"Walter is still slumbering."

He sighed.

"How's your head?"

"Still attached."

"Excellent. Anything hurt particularly bad? I can work on it now."

"No, Honey," Dr. Ziga said from the doorway. "I want you to take a break today."

"But he's awake now. If I take a break he'll have to live that much longer with the curse."

"My staff and I will keep an eye on him. Why don't you and your friends collect your things. There's a broom and a mop in the closet."

Luca nudged Nathan with his foot. "He's talking to you Mr. Food fight."

"The keys are on the counter, Mom," Nathan mumbled.

Once Nathan and Walter were up, it only took a few minutes to collect all the sleeping bags. Honey helped Luca and Walter carry everything out to the car, leaving Nathan to start sweeping up the popcorn. Honey was waiting her turn to dump her bedding into the cavernous trunk of Walter's car when a familiar black SUV pulled up beside them. Brayton and Cici climbed out. Brayton took in the bedding in her arms and the sleeping bags in the trunk and raised an eyebrow at her.

"Did you stay here all night?"

"Yep. We had a slumber party."

"With five guys?" Cici asked incredulously.

"Five friends in a hospital with the night nurse down the hall," Honey corrected. "Why are you guys here?"

"Checking on you. You weren't answering your phone, again."

"Oh, sorry. I left it in my room when I went to WOLF yesterday and I forgot to grab it when I dropped by to get my bedding."

"No kidding," Brayton said, crossing his arms.

Cici pulled a phone out of her pocket and reached around Brayton to hand it to Honey. "Your roommate finally answered it."

"Did you know Zavier before this?" Brayton asked.

"Not really. He's the one who hit on me by the bathroom but we didn't talk long."

"He hit on you and now you're helping him?" Cici asked in disbelief.

Honey shrugged. "He wasn't himself."

"How is he this morning?" Brayton asked.

"Grumpy," Luca said. "It's not our fault he fell asleep in the middle of the movie."

Honey tossed her bedding on top of the sleeping bags. "I'm going to help Nathan finish up."

"Finish up what?" Brayton asked, falling into step beside her.

"Cleaning. We got into a small popcorn fight last night." She grinned. It had been her and Luca and Zavier against Nathan and Walter and Liam. She'd managed to convince Zavier to throw a few pieces, although they'd mostly been at her.

"Are you going to stay here for a while?" Brayton asked.

"No. I need to do some homework. If you have time though, maybe you could stay and keep Zavier distracted. He's awake and that curse is still messing with him."

"You can't help his headaches the way you helped mine?"

"His head is a lot more messed-up than yours."

"How can you tell?"

He sounded like he was truly interested. It was almost like they were having a normal conversation.

"Because he still has a headache."

"Why don't you stay and fix it?"

"Because Dr. Ziga told me to take a break. Besides, you can only rub a person's head for so long. I don't want to rub him raw." It was a lame excuse, but she didn't know what else to say. Brayton thought she'd cured him with massage.

"Are you going to come back?"

"Eventually. Did you talk to your mom?"

"Yeah, she said she'd see what she could do."

They passed Liam carrying another pile of belongings out to the car. Nathan was sweeping the pile of popcorn into the dustpan. Honey started collecting the empty snack bags and soda cans that littered the room and tossing them into the pizza box.

Brayton moved to Zavier's side. "Zavier?"

"Oh great, another one. Why am I being tortured by teenagers?"

"Zavier, is it worse?" Honey asked. He sounded even grumpier than he had a few minutes ago. She would have looked into his head, but Brayton was right there.

42

"Of course I'm feeling worse. You tortured me with those stupid Iron-Man movies then stayed up half the night talking."

"You were asleep. How would you know?"

Zavier growled at her. He must really feel bad. She had to figure out a way to ditch Brayton so she could work on Zavier a little more. "Brayton, can you take this pizza box out to the dumpster? I'm going to get Zavier some fresh water."

To her very great surprise, Brayton nodded. "Sure."

She filled the pitcher from the sink in the room to give Brayton enough time to get down the hall, but as soon as she thought it was clear, she shut the door and cracked open the window.

Nathan dumped the last of the dust he'd swept up into the little trash can by the door and gave her a nod. "I'll keep Brayton occupied and I'll tell the other guys to get breakfast without you."

"Thanks Nathan."

Zavier grabbed her hands before she could touch his temples. "Dr. Ziga said for you to rest. I don't want you to wear yourself out because of me."

"I just want to look. You were better last night weren't you? I want to see if I can tell why you're feeling worse now."

"I need coffee, that's why. Why don't you go with your friends and get me some."

He was still holding her wrists. Remembering what someone had said about how using magic on a wolf without permission was bad, she pulled her hands away and put them in her lap. "All right, if that's what you want. I feel fine though. I slept well last night."

43

He touched the back of her hand. "You shouldn't be spending all your time with me. Go with your friends. I'll still be here when you get back."

"Okay."

Oddly, Brayton was waiting in the hall when she opened the door, leaning against the wall like he planned to wait there a while.

"You done?"

"Done?" she asked.

"Yeah, rubbing his head."

"Oh, I wasn't. He says he needs coffee. I'll go with the guys and get him some. Can you keep an eye on him?"

"Sure, if you bring me back some too."

"I will."

5

Honey

They went to Walter's favorite breakfast place – a little mom and pop diner that served the tastiest bacon and cheese scones Honey had ever tried. She bought scones for her and her friends, then another half-dozen more for whoever wanted them at the clinic/hospital with the prepaid card Luna Lynn had given her. Not only was Brayton's mom sending Honey to college, but she was giving her a monthly allowance. Honey tried not to use it very often, but the guys paid for her all the time, and she really appreciated their help.

Back at the clinic, she climbed out of the middle back of Walter's car after Luca. Liam, on her other side, hadn't wanted to come back and was stubbornly staying put.

Honey took the drinks and the bag of food from Nathan through the front passenger window and promised, "I'll be right back!"

"I'll go with you," Luca volunteered.

They were nearly to the door when a pickup careened into the parking lot on two wheels. A police car was right behind it, sirens blaring. The driver nearly ran them over as he haphazardly parked diagonally across two spaces right in front of the door.

"What the..." Luca started.

Honey recognized the man when he jumped down from the truck and ran to the passenger side. He had the panicky look she'd seen in enough movies that she knew exactly what was going on. The policeman parked behind him and climbed out looking thunderous. She thrust the scones at Luca. She wasn't sure what she was going to do, but it looked like the man needed help.

Dr. Ziga chose that moment to stride out of the hospital followed by a nurse with a large wheelchair. "Ah, you're here. I think that's the fastest time you've made yet." He nodded to the cop. "Thanks for escorting him, Hector."

"Escorting! He blew through two stop signs and a traffic light."

"His wife is having triplets."

"Aaaaaa!" the woman screamed from the cab the moment her husband opened the door.

"So, he was understandably distracted," Dr. Ziga said calmly, pushing the dad out of the way so he could tend to the woman.

Honey didn't see what he did because the truck door was in the way, but Dr. Ziga turned to the nurse, still very calm, and said, "Get the gurney."

The woman's poor husband looked like he was going to cry. "Is she going to be all right? Are the babies going to be all right? I'm not too late am I?"

"You are right on time," Dr. Ziga said calmly.

"It's coming!!!" the woman yelled.

46

"Yes, I see. Go ahead and push."

"WHAT DO YOU THINK I'M DOING?"

Honey wanted to watch but at the same time, she wanted to give the woman her privacy. The poor dad was wringing his hands and anxiously trying to see over Dr. Ziga's shoulder. Honey was considering pulling him away so Dr. Ziga could have more room when Dr. Ziga spoke again.

"Honey, can you see?"

"No."

"Come closer and look through the window. Watching new life come into the world is one of my favorite parts of being a doctor."

Honey stepped closer. She still couldn't see much through the passenger door because the woman's leg was in the way, but she saw the floppy gray body when Dr. Ziga lifted the baby up and laid it on the woman's chest. By then the nurse was back with the gurney and another nurse carrying a pile of blankets. The baby squawked and then let out a strong wail.

"Music to my ears," Dr. Ziga said, taking a blanket from the nurse and placing it over the mother and child. It *was* chilly outside. "We're going to move you inside now. You hold on to that little one Sarah."

A shiny, black, expensive-looking car pulled into the parking lot. Honey saw a decal with two crossed sticks circled with stars on the back windshield just before it turned into a spot beyond where Walter was parked.

"Hector, since you're here, can you help move Mrs. Richards to the Gurney?" Dr. Ziga said. "Mr. Richards, once we're clear, grab whatever you think you'll need.

47

Don't forget your phone and keys. I'm sure your family will want to hear the good news."

Honey stepped back onto the sidewalk to give everyone room. Luca stayed where he was, gazing at the scene like a little kid watching cartoons. She grabbed his arm and pulled him closer to her. "You okay there?"

"Who knew today I'd get to witness the miracle of life," he said reverently. "I wish I could hold it. I've never got to hold one that young."

"She's going to have three. Maybe you can."

Something blocked the morning sun. Honey thought the rest of the guys had decided to join them, but it was a severe-looking lady with a long, black wool coat, black hair with streaks of silver, and a black hat with maroon lining that reminded Honey of a bucket hat but more stylish. To complete the look, the woman was wearing pointy black boots with two-inch heels.

The woman lifted her chin and glared down her nose at Honey. "You are in my way."

Honey grabbed Luca's arm again and pulled him backwards with her. "My apologies."

Dr. Ziga looked up from the end of the gurney where Mrs. Richards now lay. "Can I help you?" The woman didn't smell like she was actively using magic, but the scent of magic clung to the woman like cigarette smoke does a smoker. Only a witch could reek of that much magic.

The woman turned her head sharply. Honey could see her dark eyes jerking around while she assessed the scene. "You are the doctor?"

"I am Dr. Ziga, yes. This is my practice."

"I am Silvia Cromwell, here on behalf of the Witch Council. You requested our assistance with a cursed patient."

He nodded, smiling, as if poor Zavier hadn't been waiting and suffering for two whole weeks while the woman took her sweet time. "Yes, I did. As you can see, I'm rather busy at the moment, but the young lady next to you is familiar with the case and I know would be glad to take you to our patient and answer any questions you might have."

Silvia's lip didn't curl but Honey got the feeling it wanted to as her eyes shifted to Mrs. Richards who had started taking long, deep breaths and was making a face like she was in pain. "Yes, I see." Silvia's head snapped back around and her gaze fell on Honey. "Lead on."

Luca stayed behind while Honey led the woman inside with mixed feelings. She was happy because Zavier was finally going to be healed, but sad because, well she wasn't really sad. She just wanted to finish what she had started and see if worked. Zavier's health was more important than her wishes though.

She wasn't surprised to find Cici sitting in the lobby, thumbing through a magazine, but she was irked to find Brayton in the hallway outside Zavier's door instead of watching over him. Honey didn't say anything to him with the witch behind her, but she glared at him hard before opening the door.

Zavier was sleeping, or so she thought. She waved for the witch to go in front of her, then she smelled the blood.

"Zavier!"

She pushed past the woman who had just stepped into the doorway and sprinted across the room. The blanket

49

was deep red from all the blood that escaped through the slash mark across Zavier's neck. What should she do? He looked dead.

That was the first thing. See if he was alive.

"Zavier, come on, you can't die now."

Blood was still flowing from the jagged wound on one side of his neck. She felt on the other side of his neck for a pulse but couldn't find anything. She finally pushed the bloody blanket away and put her head on his chest. His heart was still beating, but it was rapid and not strong.

She looked up at the witch who was observing her with an air of disdain. "He's alive. Can you heal him?"

"I'm not a healer. I only came to verify that he was cursed."

Brayton was standing near the end of the bed. He, at least, looked appropriately shocked. "Brayton, get Dr. Ziga, or a nurse, or anyone."

The blanket near Zavier's face was too wet to use, so she grabbed the end near his feet and put it over the wound on his neck. Not for the first time, she wished she was a healer like her mom had been. Freezing him might help but she couldn't do it with the witch standing there.

"What's your power?" she asked Silvia.

"I told you, I'm not a healer."

"I know. I was hoping you might have a power that could help."

She shook her head. "Nothing can help him now."

"Do what you came for then, and get out," she snapped. It wasn't fair. They'd been so close. Zavier didn't deserve to die.

The witch moved to the other side of the bed and put her hands on either side of Zavier's head. Her magic smelled like an electric heater that hadn't been turned on for a while.

"I'm sensing three different signatures. Have any other witches been here?"

"The Enforcer healer tried to help."

"No. I know who you're talking out. It doesn't feel like her."

"You can tell who performed magic on a person?"

She pulled her hands away and scowled down at Honey. "Have you seen any other witches here?"

"No."

Dr. Ziga and a nurse ran into the room. "Status?"

"Unconscious. He's still breathing I think."

"Ms. Cromwell, are you a healer?"

"No."

"Then please leave the room. Ailey, get some blood started. Honey, keep doing what you're doing for a few minutes while I clean up."

"What about Mrs. Richards?" she asked.

"Nurse Eileen is trained in midwifery," Nurse Ailey responded briskly while Dr. Ziga stepped out of the room again behind the witch. "She'll call Dr. Ziga if she needs help and the receptionist is placing a call to our backup doctor."

"You have a back-up doctor?"

"Several. Dr. Nahas is the closest. He works at the human hospital, but he comes here if Dr. Ziga gets overwhelmed. We also call in the pack doctors from time to time."

Zavier's face was so pale he almost matched the sheets. "Do you think he'll be all right?"

"I don't know Honey. He's lost a lot of blood."

6

Honey

Despite Zavier's attempt to slice his throat with his own claw, Dr. Ziga was able to save him. It was close. If she hadn't come back when she did, he probably wouldn't have made it. Since no one told her to leave, she watched them stabilize and stitch him up, although she stood well out of the way.

Clean-up took longer than the operation. Honey helped since all the other nurses were with Mrs. Richards. The sheets were saturated with red. She gowned up, but she already had blood on her from when she'd found him. Dr. Ziga came back to check on Zavier when the cleanup was done, but it was Honey he focused on.

"Are you all right, Honey? That was quite traumatic."

"I'm fine. Will he be okay?"

Dr. Ziga sighed. "I don't know. He lost a lot of blood. He might have damaged his brain permanently this time. Was Ms. Cromwell able to help?"

"She was only here to verify that he'd been cursed," she spit out.

"Hey," Dr. Ziga said, pulling her into a hug when the tears started flowing, "you've done wonderfully. Sometimes, despite your best efforts, things like this happen. You learn, put it behind you, and move on. He's not dead. There's still a chance he'll come out of this whole."

He held her until she was able to get her sobs under control, even stroking her hair like her mom used to. He handed her a paper towel when she stepped away.

"Sorry."

"It's okay Honey. When I asked you to follow me, I didn't mean to expose you to something like this. I want you to go home, take a shower, do your homework, and rest." He pulled a piece of paper out of his pocket. "Here's a note for your teachers since you missed Friday. I want you to take the rest of the weekend off."

"But," she waved at Zavier.

"I'll keep an eye on him and text you if he wakes, although he most likely won't. I think we should let him recover a bit before you start poking around in his head again. You can come back on Monday."

She nodded reluctantly. "What about the triplets? Did everything go well."

He smiled. "Beautifully. Two boys and a girl. Come. I'll let you take a peek. I think they're all sleeping right now."

He led her into the hall. To her surprise, Brayton was still there. He pushed off the wall and stopped in front of her. His eyes jumped from her face to the red spots on her clothes and his nostrils flared. "Honey, are you all right?"

She was suddenly so angry she was shaking. "*I'm* fine," she snapped. "The person I asked you to watch for a single hour nearly died and might be permanently damaged because of it. Leave me alone Brayton."

She tried to step around him, but he blocked her, then dipped his head like a penitent. "I know Honey. I'm sorry and I apologize." He lifted his gray-blue eyes to hers. "He asked to be left alone. I didn't see how he could hurt himself with the things in the room. It didn't dawn on me that he would partially transform."

"It should of," she hissed. "You, of everyone, knew what he was feeling."

He dropped his eyes again. "I know."

Dr. Ziga squeezed Honey's shoulder. "It's not his fault, Honey. Zavier is my patient in my clinic. If it's anyone's fault, it's mine. Besides, blaming someone only brings more hate into the world. There's enough of that already. Learn and move on."

She glared up at Brayton. "Lesson learned."

7

Brayton

"What are you staring at?"

Brayton forced himself to turn his head toward the speaker but he couldn't convince his eyes to move off the girl sitting with her friends across the cafeteria. She was smiling now, but he was certain it was only a mask.

"Nothing. Just thinking."

"Right," Cici said, plopping her tray down on the table and sitting so she blocked his view across the room, exactly where he didn't want her to.

"Just ask her out," Rhys suggested.

"What? No! I'm not interested in her like that. I'm just concerned is all."

"Are you concerned about me?"

Brayton focused on Cici. "Why? What's wrong with you?"

She shook a fry at him. "My point exactly."

He rolled his eyes and turned his attention to his plate. She was right. He had been paying an abnormal amount of attention to Honey, but only because he felt bad for what happened last Saturday. What kind of person would he be if he didn't? Besides, someone needed to keep an eye on her. Her friends were clearly not up to the task. She'd already over-extended herself once and he'd noticed she wasn't quite here usual energetic self in training. Was she having trouble sleeping after seeing Zavier's neck all messed up. He was.

Malcolm slammed his tray on the table and pulled out his chair so fast the feet squealed. Someone who didn't know him would think he was angry. Brayton knew him though.

"What's got you so excited?"

"I finally cornered that girl from the Red River pack."

"And?"

"Got myself a date."

"What about…"

"Yeah, yeah, don't get your undies in a wad. She didn't know of anyone missing."

"I doubt anyone our age would notice a man old enough to be Honey's dad going missing unless he was an alpha or somebody important," Cici said.

"Yes, I'm aware of and agree with your opinion. Just trying to make Mom happy," Brayton said with a sigh.

"The investigator really has no clue what pack Honey's from?" Rhys asked.

"No. All he's discovered so far is where her house was. Most of the neighbors didn't even realize someone was living there."

Cici frowned at him as if he were in charge of the investigation. "How is that possible? Didn't someone see them move in?"

"I guess humans aren't as observant as wolves."

56

"Brayton! I am so glad you're here! You've gone to Alpha Day before. Can you have a look at this list? Did I miss anyone?" Impeccable Charlize handed him a typewritten sheet with nearly all the lines highlighted in different colors. It made his eyes water to look at it.

"What is this?"

"It's a list of all the packs, their alphas, and the people that might come with them for Alpha Day. I'm working on the seating arrangements for the reception."

"Seating arrangements?" Cici scoffed. "Aren't we eating barbecue outside?"

"Yes, but I need to make sure there are enough tables and benches for all the alphas and their families."

Brayton handed the paper back to Charlize. "How did you get put in charge of this?"

"I volunteered. Is there anyone missing?"

He nodded at the paper. "You don't need that. Just put out twelve tables. They always use the same ones. I'm sure Captain Young knows where they are stored. All you need to do is find some people to help you move them."

She immediately started scanning the Monday crowd in the cafeteria, no doubt making a list of people in her head to rope into helping her.

"Just have Captain Young ask for volunteers to help you move everything after training on Friday. If you get a couple of people from each pack it won't take long at all."

She hugged the paper to her chest and beamed a big smile his way. "Thanks Brayton. That is an excellent idea."

"I bet she'd say yes if you asked her out," Cici commented when Charlize headed back to her table of girlfriends.

Brayton barely suppressed a shiver. "Um, no."

57

"When is Alpha Day anyway?" Malcolm asked.

"This weekend. Your parents are coming with mine. Didn't they tell you," Brayton asked.

"What? No." Malcolm got that thunderous look he always got when something wasn't going his way.

"That's when your date is, isn't it?" Cici teased.

"Yes," he mumbled.

"Think she knew?" Brayton asked.

"I'm sure she did," Rhys said, "considering it was the third time he's asked her."

"She was busy the other times," Malcolm said.

"Right," Rhys nodded.

Cici tapped her chin. "I wonder who she's targeting. The Red River alpha doesn't have any children, and the children of his betas are all several years younger than us. I bet she thinks you'll introduce her to Brayton. No offense Malcolm, but you aren't exactly the most delicious-looking piece of arm candy."

"Offense taken," Malcolm growled.

"Maybe she's trying to make the Red River alpha's brother jealous but not scare him off. You would be a perfect accessory for that," Brayton teased.

Predictably, Malcolm gave him the finger.

"How old is this brother?" Cici asked.

"Mid-thirties maybe."

"Ew, that's like seventeen years apart. He's old enough to be her dad."

"Maybe he's really handsome. Don't you girls get crushes on older actors all the time," Rhys asked.

Cici's face flared red. "That was one time and I was fifteen."

58

"You still have that poster though, right, the one with all the lipstick smears?"

Malcolm and Brayton cracked up when a ketchup-laden fry hit Rhys smack in the middle of his forehead and bounced off his nose.

"Speaking of dates," Cici said, turning to Brayton with a lingering smirk of satisfaction, "who are you taking?"

"No one."

She leaned her head on her hand and studied him. "Why not? Before we came here you were going out with a different girl every night. Now you're surrounded by hundreds of single women and you haven't been out once. What gives?"

Her scrutiny was making the skin between his shoulder blades itch. "Nothing. I haven't noticed you going out either."

She shrugged and turned back to her fries. "I haven't come across anyone I was interested in."

"Anyone who's brave enough to ask her out, she means," Malcolm jeered.

"If I wanted to go out with someone, I'd ask," she retorted.

"It doesn't matter anyway," Brayton interrupted before Cici could say whatever else was about to spill out of her mouth. "Unless I was planning to marry the girl, I wouldn't take her to Alpha Day. Me being seen there with a girl would be akin to announcing my intentions."

"What?" Malcolm croaked out right before he started choking.

"Don't worry, that doesn't apply to you," Rhys said, calmly reaching over to whack Malcolm on the back.

"Only to alpha's sons. You're just ugly arm candy like Cici said."

Malcolm glared with watery eyes. "Thanks for that."

Rhys flashed a rare smile. "You're welcome."

8

Honey

"So, Alpha Day," Luca said, plopping onto the couch beside Honey.

"What about it," she asked, pulling her calculus book out of her bag. Alpha Day was the day all the local alphas came to a party sponsored by the wolf student body. It was in two days and she was already tired of hearing about it. Charlize had been dragging Honey away after supper all week to help make decorations. She should have never let it slip that she knew how to use a hot glue gun.

"Wanna go with me?" Luca asked with a wheedling smile.

"Aren't we all going?"

"We are," Walter said, sitting in the armchair at the short end of the coffee table.

"But Nathan and Liam have dates," Luca said, then grabbed Honey's calculator.

"Really! Who?" she asked, pretending not to notice Luca's antics.

Liam's going with that Charlize girl from your pack and Nathan got asked by a girl from the Mason pack.

"Does everyone have to have a date?"

"No," Walter said, pushing his glasses up his nose and squinting at his own book. "Some people just like to show off their ability to attract the opposite sex."

"What about the same sex?" Honey waved her pencil between them. "You two could go together."

"Honey!" Luca punched her shoulder, but not hard. "No one would ever believe Walter and I were together. We're too different."

She looked between them. "No you're not. You're both kind and sweet and funny and make great friends."

Luca fluttered his thick lashes at her. "How can I keep from loving you when you say things like that."

She grabbed her calculator out of his hand. "Stop it. I'm not your fated mate. You can't go with me. What if she's there?"

He grabbed the calculator again, but she refused to let him tug it out of her fingers. He stuck his lower lip out. "What if you *are* my mate?"

She jerked her hand and her calculator away again. "Wouldn't you know by now?"

"There are various stories," Walter said, looking over the top of his book. "Some claim it was love or interest at first sight even when both people were children while others say they didn't know until they reached eighteen or even older. There's one story where neighbors were in their fifties before they realized they were fated mates."

She raised an eyebrow at him. "You sure know a lot about fated mates."

He shrugged and ducked down behind his book, "It's an interesting myth."

"It's not a myth," Luca growled.

Honey elbowed him. "He's pulling your chain. How about we all go as friends, unless you have a date Walter?"

He shook his head without looking up. "Not me. I've got too much studying to do to worry about pleasing a woman."

"That, and everyone he asked said no," Luca sneered evilly.

She punched him, hard. What could she say to cheer Walter up? He looked fine but the rejection must have hurt. "Their mistake is my gain."

Walter looked over his book again. "I didn't ask anyone, but thank you, Honey. Luca, leave her alone so she can get her homework done. Don't you have something to work on?"

Luca rolled his eyes and huffed. "Yes, dad."

She looked down at her calculator. Luca had typed in 4516604 this time. She turned the screen over and read the word. "Hoggish? What does that mean? Are you calling me a pig?"

He shrugged. "If the snout fits."

Walter nodded sagely. "You were wise to say no to him, Honey."

Her phone squeaked like a mouse. She punched Luca and tapped the screen. How did he keep figuring out her password?

"It's a text from Dr. Ziga. Zavier is awake!"

Walter put down his book. "How is he?"

"I don't know. Dr. Ziga asked if I could come by."

"Do you want me to take you?"

She slid the last of her books into her bag. "Yes, please."

Nervous was barely sufficient to describe how she felt when she walked down the hall toward Zavier's room. She'd finished with his head yesterday, and she knew the way he'd spoken to her before had been because of the curse, but part of her wondered if maybe he truly didn't like her, or maybe he was just mean.

Nurse Ailey and Dr. Ziga had their backs to her and were blocking the view of the bed.

She knocked on the door frame. "May I come in?"

Dr. Ziga waved her inside. "Please."

"How is he?"

"See for yourself."

He stepped out of the way.

The man on the bed smiled and held out a hand.

She took it and let him pull her in.

"Thank you Honey for not giving up on me."

Zavier's voice was raspy. Whether it was from his injury or because he hadn't talked in a long time she didn't know, but the sincerity of his words brought tears to her eyes.

He kissed her cheek, then kissed her forehead. "I claim you as my kin. Whatever you need, you just let me know. You can consider me your big brother or maybe a rascally uncle."

She inspected his face. His skin already had more color even though he hadn't been outside since the last time she saw him. "Rascally uncle? You're not that much older than me. Brother is fine."

He pulled her into another hug. "Perfect. I always wanted a little sister."

"Really?" Dr. Ziga said doubtfully behind her.

Zavier released her so she could stand upright again. "Well, no, not really, but I want one now and I choose Honey."

"That's sweet," Nurse Ailey said. Honey hadn't realized before how young she was. She looked about the same age as Zavier.

"Is your headache all gone?" Honey asked.

"It's perfect. I haven't felt this pain-free in months."

"And everything else?" She looked up at Dr. Ziga.

"Mostly. He doesn't remember everything, but he just woke up. It might come back to him eventually. Physically, he appears to have no lasting damage, but we haven't got him up yet. He does have a lot of muscle loss, but he's young. He should regain that with time."

"What doesn't he remember?"

Zavier rubbed his hand through his long hair. "The last several months are pretty fuzzy, but from what Dr. Ziga told me that's not a bad thing." He held out a long, lank strand of hair. "I absolutely don't remember growing my hair this long."

"Are you going to get him up today?" Honey asked Dr. Ziga.

"One thing at a time, Honey," Dr. Ziga smiled. "He's gotta crawl before he can walk."

"Crawl, eh?" Zavier flashed Honey a smile, then closed his eyes. His transformation was slow, but eventually a scruffy-looking wolf with darker hair on top of his head and back and redder hair along his belly crawled out from under the sheet.

Dr. Ziga shook his head. "Great, another patient stuck in wolf-form. I guess you guys really are related."

9

Honey

Friday at WOLF they started with a five-mile run then spent the rest of the time setting up tables and benches and tents and stacking wood for the huge bonfire. A whole row of port-a-potties lined one edge of the field. Alpha Day was also family day and coincided with human and witch families visiting campus too. When she expressed concern about humans being around all the wolves, the guys laughed at her. How was she supposed to know the college always set up another field on the other side of campus for the humans?

Between classes she helped some of her witch friends carry their things to the student union lawn. The witches were planning a barbecue as well, but they planned to sell their food and the students also sponsored an arts and crafts fair to help pay for their studies. Most of it was stuff that humans could use, like scented soaps and candles and magically grown plants (although they would never know that). Sabine was doing a make-over booth. To humans it would look like a face-painting and temporary hair-dye booth. Daegal had figured out how to package a couple of the spells he cast. Unfortunately, she couldn't see him finding very many customers for his gopher-repelling stones that reeked of dead fish or his perk-you-up charm which smelled strongly of ammonia.

Saturday was cold but clear. Honey helped Charlize and a bunch of the other girls from her pack carry the last of the tablecloths and decorations to the training grounds. Everything was ready by 10 am but people were already showing up although the food wouldn't be served until noon. Luna Lynn had given Honey strict instructions on what to wear, so she ran back to her dorm to change. The green sweater was nice – it brought out the green in her eyes, but she knew she was going to get the light-colored slacks dirty.

Two boys stood when she rushed back down to the lobby. Luca, she'd expected. Brayton was a surprise. Luca stepped forward first and took her hand with a grin that made her wonder what kind of note he was going to attempt to stick on her back this time.

"You look gorgeous."

She squinted her eyes at him. "What are you planning?"

He had the audacity to look hurt. "Nothing. You really are gorgeous. I...I'm," he leaned forward suddenly and planted a kiss on her cheek, then stepped back and bowed his head, "I am honored to be in your presence."

She turned her back to Brayton and looked over her shoulder. Brayton's face look like it was made of stone. "Did he stick something on me, a post-it note maybe?"

Brayton blinked and then glanced at her back. "No, nothing."

"I wouldn't do something like that," Luca protested.

"Yes you would and you have."

"That one time!"

"Three. Three times," she reminded him. Luckily the other guys had her back, literally.

"Oh, yeah." He offered her his elbow and grinned again. "Not today though. Today you are my queen."

"Is he your date?" Brayton asked. His voice was casual but he looked angry, as usual.

"No," she said.

"Yes," Luca said at the same time.

She rolled her eyes. "We are going as friends."

"I can't be the only one who doesn't have a date," Luca whined.

"You aren't. Walter doesn't have one."

"She can't be your date," Brayton interrupted. "She has to sit at the table with my family and unless you plan to marry her it's best if you sit with your own pack."

The look Luca gave her was more serious than she'd ever seen from him. Her stomach abruptly felt very strange. "I might someday," he said earnestly.

Brayton stepped between them and grabbed her upper arm. "Not for another four years at least. Come on Honey, Mom's waiting."

She let Brayton drag her away but she couldn't just abandon Luca like that. She looked back over her shoulder. "Come get me after we're done eating. I'd like to meet your family."

He grinned and gave her two thumbs-up.

She hadn't been near Brayton since Zavier tried to kill himself the second time. The furious anger she'd felt towards Brayton for not watching Zavier like she'd asked had faded when Zavier woke. It took too much energy to be angry.

He dragged her all the way outside, then pulled her in front of him and took a long sniff near the side of her face. She couldn't help getting a whiff of him. His body spray made her stomach flip.

His fingers tightened around her arm and he shook her. "You're wearing Zavier's mark. Why?"

She jerked her arm away. "You're going to leave a bruise."

He closed his eyes and ran his hand over his face. He looked and sounded slightly more calm when he addressed her again. "I'm sorry. I didn't mean to hurt you. Why did Zavier mark you?" His voice went grumpy again. "Does he want to marry you too?"

"No. It's nothing like that. He claimed me as kin. I'm his honorary sister."

He frowned. "Are you his sister?"

"No. When he woke up the second time, he was so glad to be free of the curse, he claimed me because I didn't abandon him."

His face morphed from angry to guilty then almost gentle. "He's awake? You were able to help him then, like you did me?"

"Yes."

"With your magic?"

She opened her mouth to try and deny it, but he touched her upper lip and shook his head. "I know you have a kind of magic instead of telepathy. It's okay. I won't tell anyone. I'm very grateful you have it. Do all your friends know?"

"Yes."

"Including Zavier?"

"I think so. He might have forgotten. I'm not sure."

Brayton started walking toward the training grounds. Honey followed him. He slowed down so she could walk beside him despite the crowd of people all going the same way.

"How is he?"

"Recovering."

"He's still at the doctor?"

"Yeah. He was stuck in wolf form yesterday. He was too weak to walk on two legs at first."

"Alpha Meyer wouldn't listen to Mom at all. He threatened to banish Zavier's whole family if she didn't stop asking him to relent. Probably better not to mention Zavier to anyone. I'm not sure what Alpha Meyer would do if he learned Zavier is recovering."

"Okay. Thank you for asking her. I'll have to thank her for trying."

"You should have plenty of time. She's excited about introducing you to all the other Lunas."

Honey scrunched her nose. "Really?"

"Yep. I'd say better you than me, but she will expect me to tag along and pay my respects too. She does this every year."

"I like your mom. She's nice."

"I know."

The WOLF training grounds were crawling with people, or actually, people were crawling all over the training grounds and the obstacle course and nearly every inch of space Honey could see. Not too far from the real obstacle course, a moon bounce obstacle course had been set up along with two smaller moon-bounces that were full of bouncy little kids. It reminded her of the time one of the girls in her gymnastic class had invited the whole class to a birthday party at her house. She'd had a castle moon bounce. It had been so much fun. Honey really wanted to go again, but she was supposed to be eighteenish and her attire was not really appropriate.

Brayton elbowed her and nodded toward the big moon bounce. "Bet I could beat you in that obstacle course."

"In your dreams, maybe." She paused and shook her head. "No, not there either."

Brayton squinted down at her. "I accept your challenge, little girl with the big green eyes."

For some reason, the fact that he'd noticed her eyes made her chest fill with, something. Words spilled out of her mouth before she completely thought them through. "It was you who challenged me, boy with the beautiful smile, but I will not hold it against you as I leave you bouncing in my wake."

He grinned. "You like my smile?"

She actually hadn't seen it that often, at least not close up. She pretended to study it. "What's not to like? You have teeth and lips and it's just crooked enough that it's not too perfect."

His eyes dropped to her lips. A strange look came over his face. In the movies that would mean he was thinking of kissing her. This was real life and he didn't even like her. Besides, it took two to kiss and she wasn't interested.

She wasn't at all disappointed when Brayton's mom called out, "Brayton, Honey, there you are. Come over here. I have someone I want you to meet."

10

Brayton

Following Mom around while she made the rounds was just as tedious as it had been every other time he'd been forced to do it. The only upside was that Honey was in the spotlight this time. She didn't seem to mind. Mom would introduce her as a rescued rogue who was now her ward and Honey would beam her smile and all the alphas and betas and lunas who Mom had been trying to convince to support her rogue project just melted. Okay, perhaps not melted, softened at least. Several of them threw complicated questions at Honey when Mom mentioned Honey's SAT score. Not a single one tripped her up. She was the perfect example of a reformed rogue. It didn't hurt that she was one of the most beautiful wolves there. He couldn't explain why that was. There were a lot of nice-looking female college students at their prime with perfect make-up and hair, but Honey somehow outshone them all.

He wasn't the only one who noticed. The high schoolers were falling over themselves to shake her hand.

One of them, a beta's son who clearly thought of himself as God's gift to women took her hand, leaned forward and very obviously inhaled deeply even though his Luna and Brayton's mom were standing right there. Honey made some quick motion with her wrist and the next moment, the boy was kneeling with his index finger bent down to his wrist.

She could have been in the middle of a posh English tea party the way she said, "It's nice to meet you too. Please don't do that ever again."

The kid's Luna looked more impressed by that than anything Mom had said.

Zavier's parents walked up half-way through their trip around the tables. Brayton and Bernadette immediately moved to block the meeting from Alpha Meyer's view.

Mom pulled Zavier's mom into a hug. "Nicole, Tom, it is so good to see you again."

Nicole grabbed his mother's hands. "Lynn, thank you for trying to help us. Is there any more you can tell us about Zavier? Is he still in the hospital?"

Mom reached behind her and pulled Honey forward. "This is Honey."

Nicole put her hand over her mouth. "Is she the one who found him the second time?"

Mom nodded.

Nicole pulled Honey into an embrace. "Oh, thank you, thank you. I wanted to be there for him but I had to obey the alpha." She took a sniff, then pushed Honey back to look at her. "You carry his mark. Are you dating? You look awfully young."

"No. When he woke up, he claimed me as kin as a way of thanking me. He called me his honorary sister."

"He's awake? That...that's," Nicole started sobbing.

Big, gruff Tom wrapped his arms gently around his wife and pulled her to his chest and spoke over her hair. "That sounds like something he would do. He was always very caring. Is there anything else you can tell us about him?"

"He's better. The curse is gone. He has a little bit of memory loss, but I think it's just for the time the curse was active. He was in good spirits yesterday."

Nicole Brandt lifted her head. Brayton had never noticed she had green eyes. They weren't at bright as Honey's but the red splotches on her face really made them stand out. "Is he still at the doctor's?"

"Yes."

"Oh, I wish we could go see him. Do you think we could sneak away," she whispered to her husband.

He shook his head. "I don't see how we can. If either one of us were to disappear for any amount of time we'd be questioned the moment we got back. My cousin doesn't take kindly to wolves who bring negative attention to our pack," he explained to the rest of them.

"It wasn't Zavier's fault," Honey said.

"We know, we know," Nicole said. "It was that Katie's fault. I never liked her."

Honey looked like she wanted to argue. Brayton nudged her and gave a small shake of his head.

"Well, I need to finish introducing Honey to everyone," Mom said. "I'll let you know if we hear any updates."

Mom led Honey to Alpha Shane, the leader of the Little pack next. He was in his fifties but looked just as powerful as some of the wolves in their prime. All the people at his table were smiling and laughing, unlike the people at the next table where Alpha Meyer was sitting. Bernadette placed herself between Alpha Meyer's fierce glare and Mom.

Alpha Shane stood. "Ah, Luna Lynn. I've been wondering when you'd come see me. Is this your ward who I've heard so much about?"

"This is Honey," his mom said proudly, pushing Honey forward. Brayton felt a twinge of jealousy, then got mad at himself. Did he want to be presented to people like he was a little kid? No.

"You've heard of me?" Honey asked. She seemed so innocent, but he'd bet his, well not his SUV, but his bike that she knew exactly what she was doing when she aimed those big green eyes at Alpha Shane and blinked those thick lashes. Alpha Shane really did melt into a pile of putty.

"Wow. Okay. I see why the boys are so fond of you."

"They're great guys. Every single one of them."

Honey finishing permanently wrapping Alpha Shane around her finger with a bright smile.

"Well Honey, if what everything I've heard about you is true, I would accept you into my pack in a heartbeat. In fact," he grabbed her shoulders, "in the event you ever find yourself without a pack, I hereby accept you into mine." Alpha Shane placed his lips right over the spot where Brayton had placed his. Brayton saw red. He didn't care if the man was an older alpha and he was just eighteen. Honey was his, he meant his packs'.

"Brayton! Stop that."

His mom's sharp words brought him to his senses. He realized he was growling, but worse, his fingers were

76

partially transformed into claws and everyone around was staring at him.

Alpha Shane lifted his hands off Honey's shoulders and held them up in surrender. "Message received. Looks like my boys aren't the only ones you've charmed."

Honey looked at Brayton with wide eyes, then back to Alpha Shane. "No, you don't understand. Brayton and I, well, he doesn't…"

Brayton grabbed her hand and dragged her away, several tables away – away from the wolves who were staring at him like they knew what was going on in his head. How could they know when he didn't know? He only stopped when Honey jerked her hand away.

"Brayton, where are you going? Your mom wasn't done. There are a few tables left."

He took a deep breath and turned to her. "It's considered a challenge when one alpha claims another's pack member right in front of them. I just needed to get away for a moment."

"Oh. He didn't really claim me though, did he? I'm still a member of your pack, right?"

"Madeline?"

They both turned. Brayton immediately recognized the man was another alpha but it took him a few moments to remember what pack he was from. Meanwhile, the man was staring at Honey like she was a ghost.

"Are you talking to me?" Honey asked.

The man blinked. "You're not Madeline are you?"

Honey shook her head.

"You look very much like someone I used to know. She had eyes like yours, except they were a different color and hair like yours too. He waved his hand around his eyebrows. "I think this part of her face was like yours too. If I didn't know better, I'd think you were her daughter, but that's…How old are you?"

"She's a freshman in college," Brayton quickly supplied. Why did all the other alphas keep noticing his Honey, er, the pack's Honey? Stupid name.

"Ah, no, you couldn't be her daughter then."

He sighed and looked so sad for a moment Brayton felt like he should comfort him. Honey stepped forward with her hand extended.

"Hi, I'm Honey."

Honey's hand looked very small in the alpha's hand.

"I'm Rory Silver, Alpha of the Red River pack." He sniffed. "You're from the Mooney pack, and Little?"

"She's part of our pack," Brayton quickly explained. "She has friends in the Little pack."

"Alpha Silver, I see you've met Honey," Mom said, quickly easing herself into the conversation. "She's a former rogue who is now my ward. She got a perfect score on her SAT and now attends college here."

"Why here and not somewhere else? With a score like that, you could go anywhere."

Brayton didn't really know Alpha Silver, but he decided right then he didn't like him.

Honey shrugged. "Luna Lynn offered me a free ride three weeks before classes started."

Alpha Silver nodded. "Very practical. It is a good college though. We have wolves coming from all over the country to attend here."

"And witches," Honey grinned.

Alpha Silver's smile faltered a little. "Yes, those too."

Mom looked around. "I see your wife, but I don't see your brother. Did he come this year?"

Alpha Silver sighed again and rubbed his chin.

Honey touched his arm. "What's wrong?"

Brayton made a note to go over basic alpha etiquette with her. One should never touch someone else's alpha unless the alpha initiated it.

"I guess there's no point in keeping this quiet," Alpha Silver sighed, "He's missing."

"Missing?" Brayton's mom exclaimed.

"Yeah, I sent him down to South America to meet with a pack there. We were working on a business deal. He never came back."

"When did he go missing?" Mom asked.

"Early August."

Brayton looked at Mom, expecting her to look back at him. She was patting Alpha Silver on the arm.

"I am so sorry to hear that. Are there any clues to his whereabouts at all?"

Alpha Silver shook his head. "No. He met with the pack and made it back to the airport. The airline records show he flew back into the states, but all traces of him just disappear after that. We can't find his motorcycle either. I'm afraid he crashed somewhere and no one noticed."

"His motorcycle?" Honey asked in a near-whisper. Her eyes were wide and her smile was gone.

"Yeah. My brother is a bit of a dare devil. He likes to travel and occasionally just disappears for days. I thought that's what this was, but he's never been gone this long."

"Is he married?" Honey asked.

"No. My mom really wants him to be though. She wants more grand kids."

79

"Oh. How many kids do you have?"

"None," Alpha Silver said wryly. "My older sister has one though."

"You've met him, Honey. Zavier," his mom said.

"Zavier? Zavier is my…friend." Honey looked pale.

"I thought I smelled him on you," Alpha Silver smiled. "Do you know how he's doing? My sister hasn't been able to tell us much."

"He's better," Honey mumbled. "Much better. What's your brother's name?"

"Mathias, although he prefers Matt or Mathew. I don't know why."

"Mathias is a good name," Honey agreed with a softer voice than Brayton had ever heard her use. "Do you have a picture of him?"

"Why, do you think you've seen him?"

Honey lifted one shoulder. "You never know."

Alpha Silver pulled out his cell phone and started scrolling. "It's not recent, but I think I have one from last Thanksgiving. Ooo, even better, I have one from last summer. We were fishing. He caught the tiniest fish. I don't know how the little thing got the hook in its mouth." He held up his phone.

Honey's face went completely white. "Oh, he's…he's handsome."

Her eyes rolled back in her head. Brayton dove forward and managed to catch her before she hit the ground. Shaking his head to hide his own shock, he quickly came up with a story, "She was so excited about today she probably skipped breakfast. Pardon us, Alpha Silver. I better get some food in her."

11

Honey

"Dad?"

"Honey, are you all right?"

It wasn't her dad. It wasn't a male voice, but she could picture him just like he was there. He was wearing a stupid hat and holding a fish about three inches long and grinning like he'd caught a whale. He wasn't moving though. It was just a picture. She couldn't stop the sobs even if she tried.

"Hey. Shh. I've got you. I'm here. Quiet now. There are a lot of ears."

She nodded her head against Luna Lynn's shoulder.

"Was he who I think he was?"

"My dad," Honey whispered.

"Here, I got some juice," Brayton said loudly.

"Thank you, dear," Luna Lynn said almost as loudly.

Honey opened her eyes. She and Lynn were in the back of an SUV. The back seat was down and the back hatch was open. Brayton and Bernadette were standing just outside of it.

Lynn handed her the juice. "Drink up. Brayton told everyone you skipped breakfast this morning."

"Smart," Honey whispered, not because she meant to. Her voice wasn't working quite right.

Brayton glanced towards the bleachers. "Looks like Alpha Meyer is about to give his speech."

"He's giving a speech?" They let the guy who'd forbidden Zavier's mom from visiting him – her aunt she abruptly realized – talk in front of people?

Brayton glanced back at her. "Yeah. They take turns. They all say basically the same thing though: welcome, thank you, it's been a great year, let's eat."

"I hope you put more effort into it than that when your turn comes around," Luna Lynn chastised.

"I like short talks," Honey said.

"We should head to our table." Luna Lynn patted her knee. "Think you're up for it, Honey?"

Honey swiped at the tears on her cheeks. What she really needed was a tissue for her nose, but she didn't have one of those and she didn't want Lynn to see her wipe her nose on her sleeve. "Yeah. I'm fine. It was a shock is all, seeing him so suddenly."

She'd said too much. Her eyes started watering again.

Lynn hugged Honey to her shoulder and handed her a T-shirt from the bag of extra clothes all the wolves carried in their cars. "It's okay dear. We have time. Alpha Meyer isn't known for his short speeches."

"That's an understatement," Bernadette said under her breath.

It took Honey a couple of minutes to calm down again. She really wished Brayton would go somewhere else while she was crying. It was bad enough she was crying all over his mom.

"Mom, how old was Mathias? I thought he was the youngest of his family," Brayton asked.

"He was," Lynn said, rubbing Honey's back. "Let me see, his sister is about my age, but she got married early. Assuming two years between kids, and that's purely an assumption, he was thirty-four or thirty-five."

"Thirty-five," Honey sniffed, then hid her head when more more tears threatened to fall while Brayton watched.

"When is your birthday?" Brayton asked.

"It's in December," Luna Lynn responded when Honey didn't. She rubbed Honey's shoulder. "I've been thinking of throwing a party."

"Please don't," Honey mumbled. "Not now. Not this year."

Lynn hugged her. "Of course, dear. Definitely next year though, it's a big one."

"You're going to be eighteen right?" Brayton said, "That means he would have been seventeen when you were born."

To Honey's surprise, Lynn didn't correct him. "You know as well as I that it's not impossible."

"Yeah, but he would have been in high school." He nodded at Honey. "Her mom would have been in high school. How did they keep that hidden?"

"Maybe they had help," Lynn said. "It's not unheard of for parents to send their teenage kids to another pack to visit relatives if there's trouble at school."

"I could understand them keeping it a secret when she was a baby," Brayton persisted, "but why didn't they tell someone when they were older? They could have made a life together. Honey could have been raised as part of the pack."

"I don't know Brayton," Lynn answered. "The Silvers have always seemed like nice people to me, but things aren't always what they seem on the surface."

"My parents are dead," Honey whispered, because talking would have set her off again. "They clearly had a reason."

His eyes met hers, then dropped. "I know, Honey."

A large body came around the side of the SUV and blocked the sun. "There you are, dear. Everything okay? Paul said Honey collapsed."

"Everything is fine, Brandon. Honey just had a bit of a shock is all." Lynn looked up at Bernadette who looked around, then nodded. Lynn wiggled her finger at her husband to get him to lean closer, then whispered, "Mathias Silver is Honey's father. We just spoke with his brother. He's been missing since August."

Alpha Brandon straightened, looking doubtful. "Are you sure? I mean with his reputation I guess I shouldn't be surprised, but he never struck me as someone who would stick around."

Lynn nodded. "Alpha Silver showed Honey his picture."

The SUV sank when Alpha Brandon sat heavily beside Lynn. "Well, that's unexpected. Are we going to tell them?"

Honey's heart seized. "No!"

"We can't," Lynn said at the same time. "Not until we know why Honey's parents hid her and why they were killed. It's clearly more complicated than a hidden affair. We need to figure out who her mother was first. If I had

84

to guess, I'd say someone in Mathias' family really didn't approve of her, but I don't know who could have held a grudge for so long. Mathias' father has been dead for years and Rory was clearly concerned that Mathias was missing. I can't see his sister ordering them killed either."

"You're right, of course." He leaned around Lynn and patted Honey's knee. "Don't worry Honey, we'll keep you safe. Did you know your father was an alpha's brother?"

She shook her head. "I didn't even know his real name."

It hurt that her parents had never told her. She knew why they hadn't. She couldn't tell anyone if she didn't know. It still hurt though.

"That's right," Lynn said suddenly. "Rory thought Honey was someone named Madeline at first. Maybe that's her mother's real name. Do you remember anyone named Madeline?"

Alpha Brandon thought for a moment, then shook his head slowly. "No. They all would have been several years behind me in school though. You could try some old yearbooks."

Luna Lynn patted his knee. "That is an excellent idea. I'll take a look as soon as we get home." She scooted out the back of the vehicle. "We better make an appearance. We don't want Alpha Meyer upset, especially since Honey has an aunt in his pack." She squeezed Honey's calf.

Lynn wasn't going to find anything in the high school yearbooks. First, Honey's mom grew up in a small town in Illinois and second, she was two years older than her dad. Honey made a note to herself to look in the college yearbooks, if the college had them. She might not know her mom's real name, but she knew she'd double-majored

85

in business and mathematics and that she'd earned her degree. Her mom had mentioned more than once that she'd had Honey after she graduated.

The barbecue was delicious. There was smoked, shredded beef with a special sauce on a soft roll, beans, coleslaw, and corn-on-the-cob followed by a piece of pie or a brownie. Honey was so full it was an effort to move when Luca appeared eager to introduce her to his family. He dragged her through the crowd hanging around the alpha tables to the grassy area half-way to the port-a-potties. There were so many families sitting and eating on blankets and tarps she could barely see the grass.

His family occupied one of the biggest blankets. There were three sisters, two brothers, two spouses, more than a few young children, and of course, his parents. She quickly discovered where Luca got his hugging tendencies from (his mom) and his irritating tendency to play with people's ring tones (his brother) and his love for children (his whole family). His mother insisted Honey sit next to her and tell her all about how they'd met, and then started asking her about her future plans.

Honey really had no idea what she wanted to do other than learn, so she blurted, "After I get my bachelors, I'm either going into graduate school or into medical school."

"Oh, you want to be a career woman. Well, you're lucky. I love kids, especially grandkids. I would be glad to watch your children for you while you go to work. I think it's horrible that so many mothers have to rely on strangers to watch their children."

"That's very kind of you," and odd to volunteer to watch a stranger's children years from now, but Honey didn't say it out loud.

"You should start while you're young. Sure, it's good to have income and a comfortable place to live, but trust me, you want to have the kids while you're young rather than waiting like so many women do now-a-days. It's easier on your body and just easier in general and the sooner you start, the sooner you can have your own grandkids."

"Grandkids?" She was only fourteen, but she didn't say that out loud either.

"Sure." Luca's mother patted her husband's arm. "I was nineteen when I got married and had my first child at twenty. I haven't regretted it for an instant."

"Wow."

"So have you and Luca set a date yet?"

"A date?"

"Yes, for your wedding."

That sound in the Disney movie where Mickey Mouse starred as one of the Three Musketeers when everything came screeching to a halt because someone said something weird happened in Honey's head.

"What?"

"What are you doing Luca?" his mom asked, peering over Honey's shoulder.

Honey jerked her head around and caught Luca frantically waving his hands.

"Luca, what is she talking about?"

Luca covered his face with both hands for a moment, then wiped them down his face. "Mom, I told you, she's just a friend."

His mom made a pfft sound. "Just a friend. Every 'friend' I've ever been introduced to is now a part of the family."

"I warned you bro," one of his single brothers smirked. "Do not introduce a girl to mom unless you plan to marry her."

Luca looked at Honey worriedly like she was a bomb about to explode. "I'm sorry Honey. My mom is...well, like that."

"It's okay Luca." Honey turned to his mom. "It was nice meeting you. I'm way too young to get married, but if I did marry Luca someday, say in ten years or so, I'll take you up on that offer for free babysitting." She popped up before his mom could protest and moved away as rapidly as she could without looking like she was hurrying.

"Honey, Honey wait." Luca caught up with her, and then went ahead of her so that he was walking backwards in front of her.

"Are you mad?" he asked nervously.

"No."

"You're not?"

"No. Should I be?" She'd told him multiple times this wasn't a date, that they were going as friends, but she was beginning to suspect he hadn't listened at all.

He shook his head and fell into step beside her. "No, not at all." He sighed. "My mother – she's a bit much sometimes. I really did tell her you were just a friend."

"Really?"

"Really," he nodded rapidly.

She decided to let it go and punched him gently. "She loves you. She just wants you to be happy. Want to go to the craft fair? I'm going to ask Luna Lynn if she wants to go. She loves to shop."

"Sure!" Luca said, blatantly relieved to be off-the-hook.

12

Brayton

"Brayton, is Honey dating that boy?"

"Not that I know of Mom."

She *was* holding Luca's hand. He nearly growled under his breath. Stupid Little pack. It was bad enough Honey couldn't seem to get enough of their boys, but to have their alpha claim Honey when he was standing right there. It was a blatant challenge. What would happen when Alpha Silver learned that Honey was his niece? Would he claim her too? He knew his dad wouldn't protest if that's what Honey wanted, but she was theirs. They were the ones who had rescued her and claimed her first.

That was one of the stranger things about Honey. Even her parents hadn't claimed her. Why? It was one of the first things parents did when a baby was born. It's not like Matt Silver's pack would have felt it. Children were only associated to the pack through their parents until they were old enough to transform, then they were claimed by the Alpha. The only danger would have been if someone discovered her and recognized their marks. Maybe

Honey's mother had been estranged from her pack, or more likely since she'd been a teenage mother, her family. Matt Silver was a strong beta though. What was he so afraid of and who had killed him, if that was, in fact, what had happened? What if it was just an accident? Maybe he'd gone by for a visit and there was a gas explosion or something.

From the way Honey reacted, she had no doubt that Matt Silver was her dad, but the man had never struck Brayton as being the fatherly type. The few times he'd seen him, he was either standing and smirking by his brother as one of his betas or flirting with all the females in sight. He'd even flirted with Mom when he and Alpha Silver had come to the house for a meeting and stayed for a meal. Maybe he was one of those guys who had multiple wives and kept them all hidden so they wouldn't find out about each other. Maybe one of the wives had found out and had taken revenge.

Whatever he was, Honey had loved him. Her sobs were still echoing in his head.

"Brayton, how's college going? Find your fated mate yet?" Grandpa's friend waggled his furry eyebrows.

"Now don't rush him, he just started college," Grandma scolded.

"Still, he's eighteen, right? What's he doing sitting here with us old people?" The old man waved his hand out to the crowd. "At his age, I would have been out there making the rounds."

"Making a nuisance of yourself you mean?" Grandpa said.

"Look at that one with the ebony hair over there. She's gorgeous. You should go say hi."

"Isn't she one of your granddaughters?" Grandma asked.

The man squinted. "Maybe. My sight isn't as good as it used to be."

The old man was totally lying, but if Brayton didn't get out of there, he knew the old man would just be the first of his parents' and grandparents' friends to try and hook him up with someone. They all wanted their child or grandchild to be Luna someday. It usually didn't bother him. What eighteen-year-old guy wouldn't want girls falling at his feet? Lately though, he hadn't really been in the mood to date anyone. Thanks to the Blue Moon fiasco, he had to get near perfect grades in all his classes for the rest of the semester if he wanted to keep his grade point average up, which meant he was studying harder than he ever had in his life.

Had Honey's grades been affected too, he wondered when she bounced up with her possible boyfriend in tow. She didn't look worried, but other than the faint scent of tears, he couldn't even tell she'd been crying earlier.

"Luna Lynn, I'm going to the craft fair. Do you want to come?"

The whole table went silent. The girl was seriously crazy or stupid. No self-respecting wolf had ever gone to the witch's craft fair. It was safer that way.

One of his mom's friends, Louise, was the first one to recover. "The witches' fair?"

"Yeah," Honey bubbled on, oblivious, "I told my friends I'd drop by. They all have booths, well most of them. Gloria is selling plants and Sabine is doing face painting and there's a booth of pretty mugs that change

91

color or hold heat or cold depending on your drink and a lot of other stuff. I helped them set up yesterday."

Louise clutched her chest. "You helped the witches?"

"Honey plays volleyball with them. She makes friends with everyone," Mom explained. She chewed on her lip for a second, then nodded. "I'll go with you. There are a couple of witches on the school board. It will be good for our working relationships if I support their students."

How could Mom even think of going after that witch cursed him and nearly got Zavier killed?

Louise grabbed Mom's hand before he could. "It's too dangerous."

"Why do you think that?" Honey asked, tilting her head like a curious bird.

Had seeing Zavier's blood pumping from his neck not been enough?

"She's a Luna. They'll curse her or put a spell on her," Louise explained.

Honey's face hardened and took on that stubborn look she got right before she ignored everything he said. "First, most witches can't throw a spell or curse someone. Out of all my friends, only one has that ability and he's not great. Second, there will be humans there, lots of humans. They won't do anything in front of the humans – it's illegal. Third, the witches won't know she's a Luna. They can't smell things the way we do. They will be able to tell we are wolves and they will probably be just as nervous as you at first, but if you act like a customer they will treat you as a customer."

"They're witches!" Louise argued.

"They're people, just like us, with different talents," Honey shot back. "They're just trying to make money to support their education. It would be against their interests to hurt anyone. Besides, I've heard witches always have the best craft fairs. I've been wanting to go to one for years."

Who had she heard it from, Brayton wondered. Her mother was a wolf. She wouldn't have gone either.

"Lynn, after what happened to Brayton, I'm not sure this is a good idea," Grandpa said.

Finally, someone was talking sense.

"That was one witch. I've met Honey's friends. They're just kids," Mom smiled, "and I work with witches all the time. It will be fine."

"Well, Lynn, if you're going, I'm going too," Louise sniffed. "I could use another mug."

Mom patted Louise's shoulder, perhaps in relief but Brayton couldn't tell for sure. "That's the spirit, Louise." She looked around. "Anyone else?"

"I will come too," Grandpa said.

Honey looked between Mom and Grandpa, then Mom again, like she was waiting for Mom to say something. When she didn't, Honey cleared her throat.

"No offense Alpha Braxton, but you are scary. We don't want to scare the witches."

"A little intimidation never hurt anyone," Grandpa growled.

Grandma patted his hand. Whereas Grandpa looked like a retired boxer who could rip your head off, Grandma looked and acted like the sweetest little old lady you could ever hope to meet, unless you made her mad, and even that was hard. "Braxton, I'm sure they will be fine. Lynn knows how to take care of herself, and she'll have Bernadette with her.

"And me," Mom's friend Selma spoke up.

"And me." That was Alicia.

"I'll go too," Brayton volunteered. Might as well. Other than the moon bounce, there wasn't much else to do.

"Brayton," Grandpa said with a warning in his tone.

"Don't worry, I won't eat or drink anything."

The eight of them set off across campus. Honey and Luca took the lead. Honey's curls bounced with every step she took. She didn't hold Luca's hand, but she laughed at nearly every word he said. Was she flirting? No one could be that funny.

The stench of magic hit before they could see the fair. Brayton wanted to hold his nose. Honey lifted hers and took a long whiff.

"I don't think I can do this," Selma said, hunching like the frightened wolf she was.

Honey turned her green eyes on Selma with concern. "What's wrong?"

"There's too much magic," Selma said. "I think I'm allergic to magic."

Honey didn't roll her eyes, but Brayton sensed she wanted to. "You can't be allergic to magic. You *are* magic." She took another deep breath. "It smells good. I mostly smell spells for healing, but there are some fun ones in there too, like color changing. That smells like crayons. There are also crafting spells. Those smell like whatever the witch is best at: clay for pottery, hot metal for jewelry, and cotton for clothing."

"You can't tell what kind of magic it is from smell," Selma scoffed.

"Honey can," Luca said. "I can a little too, now that I started paying attention."

"Honey's nose is the reason I'm not in jail," Brayton added, despite himself. "She detected the curse in my drink when no one else could. Even Grandpa didn't catch it."

"Come on, Selma. You're braver than this. These are students and their families. Our kids eat with them in the cafeteria every day," Mom encouraged.

Selma took a fortifying breath and stood straighter. "You're right. I'm braver than this." She dipped her head. "Sorry Luna."

Mom patted her arm. "It's all right Selma. The smell is a little overwhelming."

"Breathe through your mouth," Brayton suggested. "It helps."

Luca and Honey exchanged amused glances. Little twits were laughing at him but there wasn't much he could do about it.

Honey surged forward and led everyone around the building that was blocking the view.

The expanse of lawn in front of the Student Union rolled out in front of them. From their uphill position they could easily see how the fair was laid out. The outer rows of tents formed a huge square with one large main entrance. Inside, the rows were laid out in straight lines except for two perpendicular rows opposite the main entrance which looked cut-off from the rest.

"It looks like a trap," Louise commented. "They've got everyone boxed in."

"It's to control the flow of traffic and keep," Honey glanced at a couple of humans passing nearby, "non-professionals out of the restricted section."

"Those two rows by themselves?" Brayton asked.

"Yeah. You can only get in there by passing through a special tent."

"Did you go in there?"

"Yes."

"What's in there."

"Well, the vendors weren't there yet when I went in, but they sell things that only certain people would use like special pots and ingredients and," Honey looked around again, "things that are hard to hide in front of others."

"Like curses?"

Honey shrugged. "I suppose. We could probably get in if you want to look around."

"Let's just concentrate on getting through the normal part," Mom said.

Honey got more excited the closer they approached. She kept sniffing the air and asking Luca if he could smell what she did. He kept saying he could, but other than funnel cake and some kind of Asian sauce, Brayton couldn't pick out anything other than blatant magic.

A friendly-looking older woman was sitting next to the entrance, casually knitting and chatting with people when they walked in. She shot them a brief glance. The stench of magic was suddenly so strong Brayton could almost feel it. The woman turned back to the humans in front of her with a smile, but as soon as they moved on, she got to her feet and blocked their way.

"There are humans present. I won't let you cause any trouble."

Honey blasted her with a smile. "We aren't here to cause trouble. We're customers. I helped several of my friends set up yesterday and," she waved at his mom. "Mrs. Mooney is on the college board. She wouldn't do anything to harm the reputation of the school."

The woman's hard look didn't soften. "Anything in particular you are looking for?"

"Well, since none of them have ever been to the craft fair on campus before, no, but I did tell them about the mugs that keep drinks warm or cold and I'm hoping Gloria still has some of those mixed herb pots, oh and I was going to get Sabine to add some highlights to my hair."

His mom stepped forward and squeezed Honey's shoulder. "What my ward is trying to say, is that we are here to promote peace and friendship. It's been over fifty years since we signed the treaty. That's longer than many of us have been alive. Don't you think it's time?"

The woman raised a skeptical brow, "And you think attending a craft fair will do that?"

"Yes."

The woman gave a little shrug and took a step back. "I was alive when the treaty was signed. Things are much better now than they were then, but you're right, they could be better. If you're looking for Christmas gifts, my daughter is selling scarves and gloves in booth 13." She lifted her needles, "all handmade. No," she mouthed the word 'magic'.

"Thank you," Lynn said, "I will be sure and visit."

The woman shook a knitting needle in Mom's face. "If you cause any trouble though, I will use my magic against you as is my right for the defense of myself and my people."

"I understand," Mom said, still smiling.

Honey had been right not to bring Grandpa.

"Do you think she was telling the truth about making things without you-know-what?" Selma whispered after they'd entered the first row. "I can't smell anything but you-know-what in here."

"Yes, at least, *she* didn't use her power to make them," Honey replied over her shoulder. "She smelled like a thunderstorm. I think her power involves lightning, which is probably why she was the guard."

"Lightning? They can do that?" Selma squeaked.

"They can do all sorts of things. Look! Those are the mugs."

They were the strangest looking mugs Brayton had ever seen. Instead of plain cylinders with handles and maybe a picture on the side like every other mug in the world, the witches made them look like tree stumps and colorful frosting swirls. Mom and her friends were all agog about some mugs that looked like they were wearing sweaters with buttons. Why? He had no idea. He personally liked the one that looked like it was melting into the shelf, but he was careful not to admit it out loud. Not surprisingly, Honey picked a mug that was blatantly magical. It had a silly face that changed depending on what was in the mug.

13

Honey

The craft fair was just like she'd imagined it. Better actually. Lynn was having a great time and the witches seemed to like her, and not just because Lynn was buying something at every booth.

If only Mom could be there with her. Dad too, although he wouldn't have found a craft fair as fun as Mom. They'd all gone to a small human craft fair once after her dad walked through to make sure there were no other witches or wolves. Her mom had bought a colorful flowing skirt that had reminded Honey of that day every time she wore it. Honey had bought a used book for fifty cents and her dad had bought a huge barbecue sandwich that dripped sauce all over his T-shirt when he took a bite.

"Honey, what do you think of this?"

Luca held up a ridiculous-looking knitted hat with eyes that jutted up off the top and ear flaps that looked like actual ears.

"You should definitely get that. I'm sure the whole campus would appreciate the laugh every time you walked by."

He studied the object in his hands with a serious face. "You think?"

"Luca."

He nodded. "You're right." He put the hat on his fist and moved it up and down. "Look how the eyeballs bounce. I *should* get this."

She swiped it from him. "No. No you should not. Liam and Nathan will refuse to be seen with you."

He swiped the hat back. "Who cares what those two stuffed shirts think."

"You damage it, you buy it," the vendor said with her finger in the air threateningly.

"How much?" Luca asked.

"Fifty."

"Ouch." He carefully put the hat back on the dummy head and patted the top. "Goodbye, friend."

Honey grabbed his elbow and dragged him out the entrance. Brayton and Bernadette were standing just outside the tent with various bags. Brayton was frowning, as usual. Bernadette raised an eyebrow at Honey. "What did he try to buy now?"

"A hat with bouncy eyeballs."

"Here's a tip child, bouncy eyeballs are not a good fashion statement for anyone."

"It was hand-crafted!" Luca spouted.

Honey tugged on his elbow. "We'll be in the next booth."

It was another one that sold soap and candles and incense. They also had a good variety of smudge sticks.

"Ah, more soap," Luca gushed. "Maybe I'll be able to find one with a manly smell this time."

"You want one that smells like sweat, gym socks, and old pizza boxes?" Honey inquired.

"No, that is a boyish smell. I want a manly smell."

"Sweat, motor oil, and beer?" Honey asked, remembering her dad's scent after he changed her mom's oil.

Luca pointed at her. "Exactly."

The vendor, an older lady, asked if there were any special properties he'd like his soap to have. Honey wandered over to a shelf of candles while Luca blathered about soft skin and attracting his mate. Unlike most of the other booths, this one had products from several different witches. Curious if they used the same herbs her mom did, she started reading the ingredients. She was on about her fifth one when she found it – a candle made by her mom.

She forgot how to breath. Was her mom alive? Had those bodies in the fire belonged to someone else? Had her mom been wondering where she was this whole time? Mom was going to be so surprised when Honey told her she was in college.

She whirled around. "Excuse me, where did you get this?"

The vendor looked up with a frown from her conversation with Lynn, who had finally arrived from the previous booth. "I'll be with you in a moment."

"Please."

"She's with me," Lynn said to the vendor. "Don't worry, I won't go anywhere."

The witch's eyebrows were still creased but she lifted the candle out of Honey's hand and adjusted her glasses to read the label. "M&H. Oh, this is from a very talented healer," she peered at Honey over the candle, "although I can't imagine you have arthritis."

"How long have you had it?"

The vendor handed the candle back to her. "I assure you, it is still potent."

"That's not why I'm asking. When did you purchase this? Where did you purchase this?"

The woman hmm'd. "That would have been at the beginning of the summer. I put in another order for the Christmas season from that vendor, but I never received it. That's the last of my stock."

Honey felt like an elephant had kicked her chest. She knew her mom was gone. It was stupid of her to hope otherwise.

"Honey, what's wrong?" Lynn asked.

Honey shook her head and turned away to put the candle back before she started crying in front of the vendor. Luca was suddenly at her side. He took the candle out of her hand before she could place it on the shelf, then leaned close and gave the tiniest of whispers, "Your mom?"

She nodded.

"How much?" he asked the vendor.

"That's a special candle meant to relieve arthritis. It is imbibed with magic."

"How much?" Luca asked again.

"Twenty."

Luca pulled a single bill out of his wallet and offered it to her.

Honey grabbed his arm. "No Luca, it's okay."

"You should have something."

102

He didn't say it, but 'of her' was in his tone.

The woman snatched the bill. Luca offered Honey the candle. "Here. A gift from me."

She couldn't stop the tears that bubbled up as she pulled it close to her chest.

"Honey, what is it?" Lynn asked.

"It was her mom's favorite brand," Luca replied. He put an arm around Honey and turned her toward the front of the booth. "I'll take her somewhere. Please finish your shopping Luna."

Lynn stepped in front of them and opened her arms. "Come here, Honey."

Her tears burst free. Lynn pulled her close and held her until the sobs finally lessened, then she produced a handful of tissues from somewhere.

"You've had a rough day little cub. Why don't you go back to your dorm and wash your face. The girls and I will keep going. I still have a few more Christmas presents to buy."

Keeping her head down to hide all the dripping, Honey nodded, "Thank you, Luna."

"You're welcome dear."

The vendor caught her before Honey left the tent and held out a small box. "Here. Soothing soap. It's on the house. I'm sorry for your loss."

"Thank you. Sorry for crying in your booth."

She waved Honey's concern away. "It's all right. Besides, your Luna's friends kept shopping while you were crying, so it's not like you hurt my sales." She squeezed Honey's shoulder and said in a gentle voice. "I've lost loved ones too. You never stop missing them, but the ache does get better over time." Her kind words made

103

Honey want to cry again. The vendor gave her a little push. "Now go before you start again. People will think my products don't work."

Honey tried to chuckle, but it was mostly a sniff.

14

Brayton

Honey trudged out of the tent holding the candle close to her chest with one hand and a soap box and a wad of tissues in the other. The cheery smile and the bounce in her step were gone. The alpha in him didn't like seeing a member of his pack hurting. Honey lifted her face briefly to the sun and he caught sight of her eyes. Between the angle of the sun, and her recent bout of tears, her eyes were like two brilliant emeralds.

Luca put his arm around her shoulders and gave her a squeeze. "While you're washing up, I'll make you some of that tea we bought."

We.

Stupid Little pack.

"They seem awfully cozy," Bernadette commented once the two were nearly at the exit. A few seconds later, she added, "I'm surprised you haven't found a girlfriend yet. You're not bad looking."

"Thanks."

"I mean, you could have a bit more muscle and, you know, grow your hair out a little so you can do that sexy tousled look, but you're not bad."

Sexy was not a word he ever wanted to hear from Bernadette's mouth. Ever. "Let's talk about something else."

She didn't say anything for nearly a minute, and he was hoping it would stay that way, then she opened her mouth again. "What do you think of Honey?"

"What do you mean, what do I think of her?"

"I noticed you watching her."

"I wasn't watching her."

"Mmm-hmm. You still dislike her?"

"No. I like her just fine."

"Then why do you frown at her so much?"

"I wasn't frowning."

"Right."

"She's just," he shook his head, "Honey."

"Are you jealous?" Bernadette prodded.

"What!?"

"Of that boy. You only started frowning when he came around."

"Jealous? Why would I be jealous? I'm not interested in Honey." He had to clear his throat to hide the squeak he barely managed to catch.

"Mmm-hmm."

Bernadette was really annoying sometimes. He lifted his arms and the multiple bags decorating him like a tree. "I'm going to put these in the car."

She shoved the bags she was holding at him. "Take mine too. I should have my hands free anyway."

106

He sighed loudly, because, but took them. Mom only had a few booths to go and the way she was throwing money around, the witches would be fools to mess with her.

Arms loaded, he made his way to the front entrance. The old lady with the knitting needles was still there. She raised an eyebrow and wiggled a needle at him. "Find everything you needed?"

"And a lot of things we didn't," he groused.

She chuckled. "Smart woman to bring someone to carry all the bags."

"Yeah, that's my mom."

"I will say, your strength is one thing I envy about you wolves."

"Yeah, well, lightning powers are pretty cool."

She frowned. "You can tell?"

He wiggled his nose. "You smell like a thunderstorm." He wished he could smell her power like Honey could, but his nose was completely overwhelmed, not that he would tell the witch that.

She wiggled further back into her seat with a pleased smile on her face. "That's not bad. I like that. I like thunderstorms."

It should have been a nice, easy stroll up the hill and across campus the quarter mile or so to the parking lot. Nope.

He walked around the corner of Menshing Hall and into an uncomfortable ocean of alpha power. Who was right smack in the middle? Honey, of course. Worse, she was facing off against not one, but two twenty-something alphas-to-be: Damien and Deacon, Alpha Meyer's twin sons. Brayton knew who they were, but he didn't know them, know them except by reputation. It wasn't good.

Both men were looming over Honey, their big round faces bright red. Honey had her back to the wall, but her stance was the opposite of submissive. Her boyfriend, on the other hand, couldn't even hold up his head.

"Tell us b***," one of them demanded.

"No," Honey said. "Turn off your alpha power and leave us alone. This is your last warning."

She might be a good fighter, but against two full-grown men? She was going to get herself killed. He dumped the bags next to the wall and started wading through the ocean of power. If he was honest, he was pleased that he could. "What's going on here?"

"Oh look, it's the Mooney kid come to play," the twin closest to him sneered. He felt a slight increase in the force pushing against him, but it wasn't enough to stop him.

"What do you guys want?"

"Not your business."

"She's in my pack."

The man sniffed the air above Honey's head. "You sure about that?"

"Well, she was five minutes ago," he rolled his head towards Honey, hoping she'd get the message to stop antagonizing them. "Did someone else try to adopt you into their pack?"

She glared. "They want to know where Zavier is so they can hurt him."

"Ah. Idiot shouldn't have marked you. You did tell them that he only did so because you saved his life, right? That doesn't mean he'd tell you, a volunteer he only met a few times, where he planned to go."

108

"She knows something," the man farthest from him growled.

"Honey knows many things. Most of them probably useless. I doubt she even knows who you are."

"I know," Honey stated. "They're Alpha Meyer's boys. The apples don't fall far from the tree."

"Are you calling us apples?" the twin in front of her and farthest from Brayton asked.

"Is that a bad thing?" she challenged.

He didn't immediately say anything, but his power pulsed with anger after a few moments. Stumped. Point, Honey.

"Look, you and I both know fighting is forbidden on Alpha Day. Zavier is no longer a part of your pack or your concern. Let's all just go our separate ways and forget about this," Brayton tried.

"Where is he?" the man in front of Honey demanded. "Did you rogue-lovers take him in too?"

"We did not," Brayton replied.

"What about your pack, Little. Did you guys take him in?"

"N.no," Luca pushed out.

"Did another pack take him in?"

"No."

"Do you know where he went?"

"No!" Honey said. The alpha power around Brayton abruptly ceased.

"Let's go. Quickly," Honey said, running towards Brayton and away from the twins who were standing like statues. The far one was still looking at Luca expectantly. "Grab your bags. We have about thirty seconds."

She froze them. He knew it! He knew she'd used magic on his friends and him that day they captured her. "What did you do to them?"

"Come on, Brayton."

She was already sliding some of the bags onto her arms. He turned and jogged toward her. Really, he shouldn't be running away, but it would be better if the twins didn't see him standing there alone when they unfroze. "It's illegal to perform magic against a wolf."

"Unless you're defending someone."

"Actually, the law says self-defense," he pointed out.

"Well that's stupid. What if someone is attacking your child?"

"Where do we go?" Luca asked while they jogged around the corner of the building back toward the fair. "Should we go back to the fair?"

Honey had already turned left to run past the front of the building. "No. We don't want to lead those two to the witches."

"There's nowhere to hide if we head back to the field," Luca panted. "They'll catch us."

"You're the only one I'm worried about. Brayton and I can't be forced to say anything. I'll take care of them if they get too close. Let's go one building farther then head back. They'll be a little disoriented at first and will hopefully follow our trail back around the building." She took off. Luca was right behind her. With all the bags, they looked like they were running from a robbery.

Brayton didn't want to run. He wanted to confront Honey about her illegal use of magic, but he didn't really want to be around when those two idiots woke either, so he followed.

They passed the second building and turned toward the field. Luca peered around the back edge of the building ahead of them, then glanced back over his shoulder. "I can see them."

"Just go," Honey said. "We still have a lead. Run and don't look back. We'll be fine. Go!"

He gave a quick nod, took a deep breath, then sprinted out from the edge of the building as fast as Brayton had ever seen him go.

"There they are!" a voice roared. It sounded close.

Honey ran out right behind Luca. Brayton scanned for the twins when he passed the corner of the building. They were about fifty yards away and charging toward him through the green space behind the buildings like a couple of bull elephants. No, they were charging toward Honey. He wasn't even a blip on their radar.

He raced after Honey to put himself between her and the twins. That he'd been able to stand up to their power meant his was stronger, but they were at least six years older than him so it probably wasn't by much. Still, he should be able to at least slow them down.

It didn't come to that. Honey and Luca were amazingly fast. They pulled ahead of him and well ahead of the two behind him. Brayton stopped worrying once they reached the parking lot. If Luca was smart, he'd plant himself somewhere close to his alpha.

Brayton slowed to a walk when he reached the parking lot. Wolves were everywhere. Unless Damien and Deacon were idiots, they wouldn't try to pick a fight in front of everyone. He made sure they weren't following him though before he headed to the SUV to stash the bags he was carrying. For all he knew they *were* idiots.

Arms empty, he made his way onto the field. After only a few seconds, he spotted the twins standing on either side of their dad who was sitting at the head of his alpha table like a king. All three of them were glaring towards the Mooney table where Luca and Honey now sat with a pile of bags in front of them. Brayton's dad wasn't there. He was talking to some guys near one of the grills, but there were plenty of other wolves around the table. Luca's arms and lips were flapping excitedly. Honey was leaning against her arm which was leaning on the table so she could watch him in admiration, Brayton assumed. He couldn't see her face. Honey's other friends, Liam and Nathan and Walter, were there too with Charlize and a girl he recognized from training.

"Hey, Brayton," Malcolm said at his elbow, "This is Cyrus." He had his arm around the redhead he'd been drooling over since the beginning of the semester. She looked up at Brayton through her long eyelashes and dropped a come-hither smile that normally would have made his pulse race. Instead, he instantly disliked her. She was supposed to be Malcolm's date.

"Hey." He gave her a nod and turned back toward the scene in front of him.

"What's going on?" Malcolm asked. "I saw Honey and Luca run in like someone was chasing them, but nobody followed."

"Someone *was* chasing them. Honey managed to antagonize Damien and Deacon."

"Oh, man. Does she never learn?"

"Those are the alpha twins from the Wolfborne pack, right?" Cyrus asked innocently. Brayton was sure she knew

112

exactly who they were, how old they were, and their current availability.

"Yeah. Beasts, both of them," Malcolm said, "They don't know how to properly treat a woman, not like me."

"What did she do? Was she *flirting* with them?" Cyrus sounded disgusted and shocked as if she'd never stoop that low. Other than the red hair, Brayton couldn't understand what Malcolm saw in her.

"No." Cyrus didn't need to know Honey's peculiarities. "She was being her usual stubborn self." Malcolm would know what that meant.

"They were trying to use their alpha power on her? Why?" Malcolm asked.

Brayton sent him a 'shut-up' glare. "Because they want to know where Zavier went and they think she knows." The sad thing was, all they had to do was call the doctor. Maybe he should call and warn Dr. Ziga's people not to release any information on Zavier over the phone.

"Zavier as in Zavier Brandt? Isn't he the one that nearly killed a couple of people a few weeks ago? I thought he was in jail," Cyrus said.

"No." Brayton couldn't think of a reason not to set her straight along with all the girls she would probably tell. "Zavier was cursed. He didn't mean to hurt anyone. All the charges were dismissed."

"Why would they think Honey knows anything about him? Wasn't she a rogue until recently?"

The way she said rogue, like it was the worst possible thing someone could be, really irked him. "Honey helped prove he was cursed."

At his table, Alpha Meyer stood, his eyes still locked on Honey.

"Excuse me. Malcolm, can you find Dad or Grandpa and tell them to head to our table?"

"Sure."

15

Honey

She shut her eyes. Luca's detailed, yet rather unorganized recounting of their adventures at the craft fair faded into the background noise. Speeding up both her and Luca's molecules so they could outrun the mad alpha twins had sapped all her remaining energy. She just wanted to go back to her dorm and nap, but she couldn't leave Luca unprotected. Now Liam and Nathan and Walter were there too.

"Excuse me, I don't believe we've met."

She jerked her eyes opened. How long had she been sleeping? She lifted her head and looked around. A few people were watching her, but most of them were looking at something behind her.

"Honey, right?" a smooth masculine voice asked behind her. It was too smooth, like thick oil.

She looked over her shoulder. A man of medium height and slightly over-medium weight stood not three feet from her. His two sons towered over him, one at each shoulder. "Yes, and you're Alpha Meyer, right?"

He stuck out his hand. "That's right. I heard you're Luna Lynn's new ward. Thought I'd introduce myself since she didn't bother."

Honey didn't want to touch him, so she faked a yawn that led to a real yawn and lasted so long a normal person would have dropped his hand. Alpha Meyer didn't. Now she really didn't want to touch him.

"Sorry we missed you earlier. I fainted before we got to your table and you woke me up just now. I shouldn't touch your hand. I might be coming down with something."

"I'll wash it."

"I don't want to risk it though. You gave a nice speech earlier."

He finally dropped his hand but kept the pleasant look on his face. "Thank you. Rumor has it you are a former rogue who was adopted by the Mooney pack and are now going to college on scholarship."

"Yes."

"How nice for you. My sons tell me you know Zavier."

At least he got to the point. "Zavier Brandt?"

"Yes," he said through teeth clenched behind smiling lips.

"I know him."

"How do you know him?"

"He sliced his neck open. I stopped the bleeding."

"You're a nurse?"

"No. I was considering going pre-med and Dr. Ziga let me follow him around."

"Where is he now?"

"Dr. Ziga is probably at work."

116

"No, Zavier," Alpha Meyer growled.

"None of your business."

He started to swell. The people all around her bowed their heads like they were too heavy to hold up. Bully.

"You know something," the alpha declared.

"Nothing I'm going to share with you."

He swelled even larger. "Tell me."

"No."

"How are you resisting me?"

"Maybe I'm a stronger alpha then you."

He growled and lifted a hand that was already part claw. She shouldn't have said it, especially since she knew he was sensitive about his alpha power. Her mom would be disappointed in her. She was disappointed in her. It was something a bully would do. She didn't think she deserved to be sliced open though.

She couldn't freeze her way out of this one. There were too many people around; in particular, too many wolves with noses sensitive to magic. She couldn't fight either, not easily. She was sitting in the middle of a bench with three big alphas behind her, ready to attack. Maybe she could dive under the table?

"Don't. There's no fighting on Alpha Day and she's a minor in another pack. You'd be paying penalties for years."

She'd never been so glad to hear Brayton's voice.

"Stay out of it, runt," one of the twins snarled. He swelled up like his father, but she didn't dare take her eyes off Alpha Meyer to see what he was trying to make Brayton do.

Alpha Meyer's hand was still poised to slash her, but it hadn't moved. She dipped her head briefly. "I apologize. I shouldn't have said that about your power. I'm not an alpha. My brain just doesn't respond to alpha commands in a normal way."

"How does it respond to a beating?" the other twin asked threateningly.

"About like you'd expect, I suppose." She threw in a half-grin hoping to diffuse the situation. "Look, I know you hate Zavier, but he's no longer your concern. You kicked him out of your pack. Consider him gone."

Alpha Meyer's hand was still raised. "He claimed you. He'll be back."

She scrunched her nose. "Not that like. He claimed me as kin, like a cousin. He knew I...I'd lost my parents and..." she dropped her head. Would the tears never stop?

The smell of Brayton's body spray got stronger and something touched her shoulder. "And Honey was the only person who didn't give up on him." He spoke like he'd just ran up a mountain, but she was impressed he was speaking at all considering the way everyone else around the table was acting. He rubbed his hand along her shoulder, making her want to simultaneously turn into him and let the tears come again and turn away so he wouldn't see her cry. She'd cried enough for one day. She grabbed a spare napkin from the center of the table and dabbed at her face.

"You know where he is." It was a statement, not a question.

She took a moment to blow her nose before answering. "Yes." She was surprised he didn't know.

"Tell me."

"Why?"

118

"He's a rogue with alpha powers. He's dangerous. He's already tried to kill people once. I can't have a former member of my pack going on a killing spree."

She was so tired, she would have loved to lay down on the hard bench and sleep, but hearing his stupid excuse caused her temper to flare. "He was cursed. He didn't mean to hurt anyone. He's only a rogue because you made him that way. If anything happens, it's on you."

"Exactly," Alpha Meyer said triumphantly. "Now you understand why I need to find him."

"Are you going to accept him back into your pack?"

"He tried to kill people. I can't have a murderer in my pack."

"He. Was. Cursed." How could someone be so thick-headed?

"*Is* cursed. **Is**. You have to break a curse to get rid of it. The witch's council said there was no way to break it."

"You spoke to them?" That surprised her.

"Of course. What kind of alpha do you think I am?"

She did her best to keep her face blank.

Alpha Meyer shook his head, looking almost amused. "Despite what Zavier might have said about me, I am a good alpha. I care for my people. That includes putting them down if they become a danger to themselves and others."

She would have pointed out that he not only kicked Zavier out of his pack, but he had also prevented Zavier's family from visiting, both of which were not marks of caring in anyone's book, but given her current situation, she decided it was better to stay quiet. She even bit the inside of her lips to keep them closed. Her thoughts must have shown on her face.

"You're wondering why I kicked him out of the pack. I had to. I didn't want the curse to spread."

She wanted to tell him he was an idiot – it wouldn't have spread, but she tamed her response into a question. "Why did you think it would spread?"

"I wasn't sure, but I couldn't take the chance." He shook his finger between his head and his son's. "We're all connected. Can you imagine a whole pack with a curse?"

It would be like a horror movie where everyone attacked each other. Not that she'd ever seen one since her mom didn't like horror movies. Fixing all those minds...she shivered just thinking about it.

"Exactly. You see now why I need to find him. If he joins with another pack, think how many people could die."

"That would only happen if he is, in fact, still cursed and the curse can spread. There is no evidence of either."

"But if I'm right, a lot of people will die and it will be your fault."

What if he was right? What if she hadn't broken the curse? What if Zavier found another pack and it spread? No. Brayton was okay. He'd been cursed for weeks during which time he'd transformed in class and used telepathy with his pack. None of them had headaches. She'd scan some heads, just to make sure, but Alpha Meyer had to be wrong.

"You didn't see him after he tried to kill himself the second time. He was better. His headache was gone. He wasn't depressed anymore. He was happy, or as happy as he could be. Couldn't being near death have broken the curse?"

"Are you willing to risk it?" Alpha Meyer challenged.

She lifted her chin. "I am."

"Alpha Meyer, care to explain why you're pushing your power onto my people?"

She could literally feel Alpha Brandon on the other side of the table. Maybe her body was finally starting to recognize alpha power by feel like a normal wolf instead of by sight. Around her, everyone started popping up like wilting flowers after a good rain as his power released them from Alpha Meyer's.

"Just trying to get information about a rogue."

"You mean Zavier?" Alpha Brandon stated.

"You know who I mean."

"We have no information for you. Now please leave my people alone before I call the Enforcers. And," Alpha Brandon's voice changed from the polite one Honey had always heard to something much more dangerous. "don't ever use your power on or question Honey or any of my members the way you just did. You are to stay away from them." Alpha Meyer bent like something heavy had fallen on his shoulders. His sons bent even farther. Without another word, they turned and walked away, but the look on Alpha Meyer's face was nasty.

"Everyone all right?" Brayton's dad asked.

"Yes, Alpha Brandon," everyone chimed around her, even Luca.

"Honey, you okay?"

"I'm fine."

"Where did you leave my wife?"

"Here! I'm here Love. Oh, that was so much fun." Lynn stopped at the table with a bag in each hand, a bright grin, and rosy cheeks from the walk in the chill breeze. All the women with her, except Bernadette, were smiling and

121

chatting and swinging bags like they'd just had the best time of their lives. Bernadette looked like she'd be glad to stab someone if they stupidly gave her the opportunity.

"How much did you spend?" Alpha Brandon sounded like he was amused rather than upset.

"I got almost all my Christmas shopping done and met a lot of nice people. I should have done this a long time ago."

"You bought magical gifts for everyone?" he asked skeptically.

"Not magical. Made by magic, although there are a few things that could be considered slightly magical. Did you know they could make mugs for couples?"

"A couples mug?" He looked as confused as Honey had until she smelled it. It smelled like crushing teenagers.

"It works better than oysters." Lynn's smile got even broader. "You just add your favorite drink and share it with the person you love."

"Really?" an older man whose name Honey had forgotten, asked. The woman next to him stuck her pointy elbow in his side.

"Yes. She's probably out by now. Those go really fast and the spell only lasts a year so she gets a lot of repeat buyers."

"That's convenient," someone muttered.

"Isn't it? Lynn gushed. "I thought it was a great business idea."

Brayton tapped her shoulder. His hand had fallen away around the time his dad had appeared. "Hey, ready to lose?"

"What?"

"Obstacle course. You challenged me, remember?"

"Did I?" She wanted to run the obstacle course, she really did, but she was so tired, she'd probably fall asleep while standing in line.

"Yes, come on. Let's see if you can live up to that big mouth of yours."

"Maybe later Brayton." Would it be weird if she put her head down and slept at the alpha table?

"Come on, you can't back out now." He grabbed her shoulder again and tugged backward so hard she nearly fell.

Walter grabbed Honey's arm before she toppled over, then after seeing her face, slid onto the bench beside her and pulled her toward his shoulder. "I think Honey has had enough fun for today. I'm sure there are lots of people over there who would like to challenge you Brayton."

"Leave her be, Brayton. She looks worn out," his dad said.

If Alpha Brandon said anything beyond that, she never knew. She fell asleep.

16

Honey

Sunday after church, Walter and Honey dropped by to visit Zavier. To Honey's surprise, Chloe, her former bodyguard, was in the lobby, reading a magazine.

"Did something happen?" Honey asked, walking up to her.

Chloe put down her magazine and stood to stretch. "You could say that. Alpha Meyer came by looking for Zavier yesterday. Dr. Ziga's people had to lock the place down and call the Enforcers to get him to leave. Dr. Ziga put out a request for some security. Since I'm still between jobs, I came. There are a couple of guys from Dr. Ziga's pack around too."

"What happened with Alpha Meyer after the Enforcers came?" Walter asked.

"He was warned to stay away. The hospital is neutral ground, even for rogues."

"Do you think he will stay away?" Honey asked.

"Away from the hospital, yes, but I'm pretty sure he's got people watching. The moment Zavier tries to leave he's in trouble."

"Won't the Enforcers help him?" Honey asked.

"He's a rogue," Chloe said as if it explained everything. Maybe it did.

Leaving Chloe in the lobby, Honey and Walter went to visit Zavier. He was still in wolf form, but his coat looked shinier and thicker, and he was stronger. The first day he'd only walked around a few steps before collapsing back into bed, but today, he was literally jumping off the furniture. Dr. Ziga appeared at Zavier's door a few minutes after she and Walter arrived and took a pained look at the huge wolf standing on the bed. "Please see if you can convince him to change back."

"On it," Honey chimed, showing him the shopping bag she carried. "Walter and I went shopping. We got him some clothes."

Zavier jumped off the bed and jabbed at the bag with his snout. She opened it so he could see. "Just some sweatpants and underwear and a couple of T-shirts and a hoodie. I think you are about the same size as Walter. I didn't know your shoe size so I got some slides. We can go shopping again once you're dressed."

His eyes were shiny when he looked up to her. She dropped down on her knees and hugged him. "I figured that was part of the reason you hadn't changed. No one likes hospital gowns."

"Humph," Dr. Ziga complained, but she knew he was joking.

"We'll wait in the hall so you can change."

125

Twenty minutes later, Zavier opened the door. His hair, damp from the shower, was still long but he smelled like soap and new clothes instead of body odor and booze, the way he had when she'd first met him. He looked a lot better too, almost healthy, although he was still too thin and pale.

"Well?"

She couldn't help herself. She threw her arms around him. She was 5'7" but like Walter, Zavier towered over her. "You look so much better. I especially like the smile."

He gave her an excellent hug back. "I feel that much better. Never thought I'd ask someone this, but do you happen to have an extra hairband?"

She stepped back out of his arms with a laugh and slipped one of the extras she always wore off her wrist. "I do. I could braid it for you if you want."

"That won't be necessary," he said quickly.

"Oh good," Dr. Ziga said from the end of the hall. "I can finally get my room back."

"What, you have someone else looking to rent it already?" Zavier asked.

"Funny. Don't go anywhere. I want to give you one last check-up before I release you."

"You're going to release him tonight?" Honey asked.

"He's walking, he's talking, and he has the makings of a nice man-bun. There's no reason for him to stay."

Zavier sighed.

"But there are people waiting for him outside," Honey argued.

"I'm aware, but he's also got some friends with a car, am I right?"

"Where should we take him?" Walter asked.

"You can just drive me out in the country somewhere and drop me off. I'll head to Yellowstone."

Yellowstone wasn't a bad idea. A lot of the land in Yellowstone was unclaimed or open to rogues and it was less likely he'd get shot by humans in a national park. On the other hand, rogues were looked down upon everywhere and the Yellowstone packs had fearsome reputations. Her dad had recommended that she not go there, but Zavier might be okay once he got his strength back.

"That's a long way," she pointed out.

"I've got time."

"Yeah, but you just got back on your feet. You should buy a ticket. It will be a lot easier and you won't have to worry about crossing pack lines since you'll obviously be traveling through."

"I'm a rogue."

"So was I."

He looked at her in surprise. "You were?" His face fell. "I forgot. You lost your parents, didn't you? That's why you're Luna Lynn's ward."

"Yes."

He pulled her into another hug. "I'm sorry, I can't remember much of the last few weeks or months. Did you tell me what happened to them?"

"They were murdered."

"Oh. Can I ask more questions or should I stop?"

"It happened at the beginning of August. They were killed in a fire but I don't know who did it or why. That's all you need to know."

He kissed the top of her head, then laid his head on top of hers. She wanted to tell him he was truly her cousin, but she was already tearing up and he needed to focus on getting away.

"I'm sorry that happened."

"Me too," she sniffed.

He squeezed her tighter. "I meant it. We are family. I am here for you."

"Even when you make it big in Yellowstone?"

"Always. You can even come visit. I hear it's beautiful there."

"A ticket is not going to be cheap and it doesn't look like there are any available for today," Walter said.

"What kind of tickets are you looking up?" Honey asked, stepping back to look at his screen.

"Plane."

"Try train or bus. He'll probably have to go through Chicago no matter what he takes, but there are several buses that run between here and there every day. He'll be able to get out of town tonight or tomorrow at least. I have some cash cards."

"I don't need your money, Honey. I have some."

"You do?" Walter asked.

"Yeah. I was saving up for a house before I got sidetracked. There's enough to help me get started somewhere new after I take care of my hospital bill."

"That's wonderful!" Honey said. She'd thought he was destitute. "I wish you didn't have to go so far away though."

"It's better this way. Alpha Meyer holds grudges and he's never liked me. If any of the local alphas accept me into their pack, he'll make things difficult for them. It's safer for everyone if I go far away."

"What if someone just marked you as belonging to a pack but you still left," Walter asked. "That would be better than going anywhere as a rogue and Alpha Meyer would never have to know."

"Maybe, maybe not. I know someone who can send me a list of all the packs in the Yellowstone area. I'll call them up one at a time and explain my situation. I'm hoping one of them will give me a chance. If not, I'll try somewhere else. If I go as a rogue, I'll be completely unfettered."

"Yeah, but some of them kill rogues on sight," Walter argued. "Besides, it might take a while and the bond will keep you sane."

"Concerned about my mental state are you?"

"With good reason."

"Keep him sane?" Honey asked.

"Yeah. That's why rogues are put down," Walter said. "They go insane after a while and once they reach a certain point they can't come back."

She'd heard plenty of comments implying rogues were mentally unhinged, but she'd assumed they were just stories or that some homeless wolves had mental issues like some homeless humans did. She hadn't realized being a rogue actually messed with a wolf's mind.

"How long can a wolf go without being a part of a pack?" Honey asked.

"Technically, years," Walter answered, looking more concerned than she liked while he observed Zavier, "but even after a couple of weeks, they start to feel the effects. A lot of them become depressed and start looking for ways to lose themselves."

She spun around to touch Zavier's chest. "You can't go as a rogue. I fixed everything but I don't know if it will stay that way. A bad knock could send your molecules all spinning the wrong way again and you've already been weeks without a pack."

Zavier raised an eyebrow at her. "My molecules?"

She shrugged, "It's how I envision it."

Zavier let out a long breath. "There's nothing that can be done. I have no doubt that Alpha Meyer will be keeping a close eye on the other alphas."

"Why does he dislike you so much?" she asked.

"Because I'm a stronger alpha than he is."

"What?" Walter exclaimed.

"My mother is the daughter of an alpha and my dad is Alpha Meyer's cousin. He's powerful enough to be alpha himself, but it just worked out that he is a beta. At three I could already out-alpha Meyer's sons. I have no interest in taking over his pack, but he is paranoid."

"Wait, if you're an alpha, can you be a rogue? Can't you just be your own pack?"

Walter shook his head. "It doesn't work that way, Honey. You can't be a pack of one, although he could start his own pack. He'd only need one other person, although more would be better."

"I'll do it. I'll be your pack," she told Zavier.

Walter shook his head again. "No Honey. You are Luna Lynn's ward. If you have a bond to a different pack someone will notice. It's bad enough you're already carrying Zavier's mark."

"I am?"

Zavier's shoulders sagged. "Sorry about that. I wasn't thinking when I claimed you as kin."

"That's okay. I'm glad you did. I'm still part of the Mooney pack though, right?"

"Yes," Walter said.

"Wait, does that mean if I kissed him on the forehead, he'd carry my mark?"

"If you meant to mark him, yeah, but it would be faint because you're not an alpha," Walter answered.

"Huh. Okay, so all he needs to do is find a couple of other rogues and make his own pack."

"No. He needs stable people," Walter explained. "Well-established alphas can handle wolves who've been rogues for a while because the rest of the pack helps stabilize them. If he were alpha to a group of rogues, they'd all bring him down."

Gah. "What about Brayton? He's a future alpha and he's already here. Could he claim Zavier for the Mooney pack?"

"He could claim him for his own pack, but not for an already established pack," Walter said. "If he claimed Zavier he'd be starting his own pack and splitting from his father's."

Why was this so difficult?

"So, we need to find someone who is currently part of a pack but won't mind switching to a pack of two."

"And losing all the benefits a pack brings," Walter added.

"And either willing to come with me or suffer being far away from their alpha for an extended period of time," Zavier said, "which means they need to have a strong support base such as a large family."

She couldn't think of a single person who fit that bill, not that she knew a whole lot of wolves, but many of the

131

ones she did know were going to school at the expense of the pack. They'd lose their support if they switched packs.

"I'll do it," Walter said. "I have a big family and our pack is so large, I doubt Alpha Shane will mind."

"Won't you lose your scholarship," Honey asked.

"No. It's through the college, not the pack."

"Are you sure about your alpha?" Zavier asked. "If one of the Wolfborne switches packs and tries to visit their family, Alpha Meyer won't let them on the grounds."

"Really?" Honey asked. "What about people who marry into other packs?"

"They either remain a Wolfborne or their families have to go visit them."

She made a face. Alpha Meyer was truly a bully.

"Alpha Shane won't mind," Walter said confidently. "He probably won't even notice for a while since I'm at school."

"You should tell him what's going on first," Zavier said, "and make sure he agrees to take you back once I find another pack."

"Right. Good point. I'll call him right now. He doesn't have anything against you, does he?"

"Not that I'm aware of."

Walter waved his phone. "Pardon me for a few minutes." He went into Zavier's room and shut the door.

"One more question," Honey said, already dreading the answer, "won't other alphas be able to detect you're an alpha with a pack yourself? If so, won't they be unwilling to accept you into their pack?"

"Whether I have a pack of my own or not, they'd know I was an alpha. I just have to find someone who understands."

132

"May I look into your head again before you do this, just to be safe?"

"Sure."

She took her time, looking over and feeling every molecule. She couldn't find a single one that felt wrong. Alpha Meyer was wrong. He had to be.

"Okay?" Zavier asked when she finally put her hands down.

She nodded just as Walter stepped back out into the hall. She thought he had bad news based on his serious expression, but he gave her a wink when he caught her eye. "Alpha Shane agrees and says he would be glad to take you into his pack, Zavier, but this will be safer for everyone, as you said. He said he knows a couple of good alphas in the Yellowstone region. He's going to text me their numbers. He also said he's glad you're feeling better. He knows your dad was very worried." Walter took a deep breath. "I do have one condition before we do this."

"What's that?" Zavier asked.

"I get to help you name our pack."

"How about the Brandt pack?"

Walter shook his head violently. "No. That sounds too much like the Brat pack. I was thinking something mysterious like the Shadow Pack."

"There's already a Shadow Pack in Arizona," Zavier said.

"It was an example. It's a cool name."

"You should have one to reflect both of you. How about 'The Tall, Skinny Dudes Pack'," Honey quipped.

They both stared down their noses at her.

"The Honey pack?" Zavier asked, "since Honey is the reason we are all here?"

133

Walter scrunched his nose. "That sounds like a pack of lovers." He waved his finger between himself and Zavier. "Not happening."

"How about the Broken Curse Pack, or the Curseless," Zavier suggested.

"That's...not bad," Walter said thoughtfully. "How about the Uncur-sed Pack?"

"That would just tempt the witches," Honey teased.

"It's not like we're going to register the name," Zavier said.

"How about the Sticky Curse," Walter said, "since honey is sticky."

Honey glared at him with her hands on her hips. "You're saying I'm a curse?"

"No," Zavier said flatly. "We can decide on a name later."

"You can call it the Nameless Pack for now," Honey suggested.

Walter gave a single nod, "I like it."

"Well then," Zavier said, putting his hands on Walter's shoulders, "I welcome you to my nameless pack Beta Knapp." He pressed his lips to the center of Walter's forehead.

It barely took a moment. Zavier stepped back and dropped his hands. Walter immediately rubbed his forehead but avoided where Zavier's lips had pressed.

"Beta?"

Zavier shrugged. "All alphas need at least one beta and since you're the only other member..."

Walter nodded, "I'm it by default. Nice."

Honey threw one arm around each of them. "Congratulations to you both."

134

"I don't know if I'd go that far," Zavier said, "but thanks Walter. I really appreciate what you are doing for me. I'll try to find another pack as soon as possible."

Walter waved his hand dismissively. "Take your time. This is probably the only chance I'll ever get to be a beta, and a young one at that." He pushed his glasses up his nose the way he always did when he was thinking. "I wonder how young the youngest beta ever was. I'll have to look it up."

Honey wrapped an arm around one of Zavier's. "Now, how are we going to get you out of here?"

"I've been thinking on that," Dr. Ziga said, coming at them from the end of the hall. "So far I've come up with a fake arrest, a switcheroo, crowd-hiding, and the classic, throw him out in the garbage. Unfortunately, he's really too big to stuff into a bag and then into your trunk."

"Seriously?" Zavier said.

"Leave the escaping to us," Honey said and pushed Zavier toward the door to the room where Dr. Ziga was now waiting. "You stick to doctoring."

"Do you know how many people Dr. Meyer has watching the clinic?" Walter asked.

"At least two," Dr. Ziga replied.

"What will they do to him if they catch him?" Honey asked while Dr. Ziga followed Zavier into the room and shut the door.

"Kill him," Walter said bluntly.

"In public? Right out in the open?"

"Unlikely, but it is permissible to kill a rogue in public if he's considered a threat," Walter continued. "Zavier's lucky he didn't get shot in the club. In this case, his old pack legally can't kill him until he's on pack grounds, but we're talking about Alpha Meyer here."

"Think he's got a sniper out there?"

"You watch too many movies Honey, but yeah, he could, or at least someone who has a very good shot."

"He belongs to another pack now though."

"An unregistered one consisting of two people," Walter pointed out. "All they'd have to do is kill me."

She didn't even want to think about that. "Will the Enforcers help him now that he's not a rogue?"

"Considering we haven't paid any pack dues, unlikely."

"We need to get him out of here without them knowing he's gone or where he went." She looked up at her friend. His jaw was a little squarer than Zavier's and his hair shorter, but they were both tall and skinny, or slim, in Walter's case. "Did you bring a hat?"

"What are you thinking?"

"You and Zavier could switch clothes. I can leave in your car with him and take him to the transit center in the city. After an hour or so, you could walk back to the dorms."

"It might work except if they're fooled by the first switch, they'll probably think I'm Zavier when I step out of the clinic in different clothes and either shoot me or try to capture me, in which case, they'll discover that Zavier now has a pack and maybe even use me as leverage to get to him. Alphas have a responsibility to their pack members. Also, no one drives my car but me."

"He's your alpha. If there's one person who is allowed to drive your car, it should be your alpha."

"Yeah, but who's going to bring it back?"

"I can. I know how to drive."

"Do you have a license?"

"No, but I can drive. My parents started teaching me as soon as I could reach the pedals."

"No."

"Well, how about once you get back to the dorms, you have Liam drive you to the station to pick up your car. I'll guard it until then."

"Funny Honey. Assuming all that works, I already see a major problem."

"What?"

"If they follow me from the dorms and see me get my car which I didn't drive, they'll know you had something to do with his escape. Alpha Meyer will be after you."

"I can protect myself."

"I know, but it's better if we keep your involvement anonymous."

"Do you have a better idea?"

"Possibly. Let's go talk to Chloe."

17

Honey

"See anybody?" Walter asked for the hundredth time while he made a slow turn into the parking lot next to his dorm.

"Nope," Honey replied scanning the parking lot and looking behind them again. As slowly as Walter drove, if anyone had been following them back from the city after Chloe and Horatio dropped off Walter in the Enforcer van, it would have been obvious.

"I feel like that was too easy."

"Easy?" she squealed. "I thought for sure someone was going to shoot Zavier when we walked out to the car, then we had to find a place to hide while still being able to watch for the bus. It was nerve-wracking."

"Uh-huh. Honey, you have nerves of steel. It's just weird that nobody followed you or me. Are you sure no one followed Zavier onto the bus?"

"I'm sure. There's no way they could have known where he was going. I snuck out of the car in an alley and bought the ticket at the counter while he drove around."

"And you saw him get on the bus."

"Yep, and watched it drive away. He waved to me. I gave him your number. He said he'll call as soon as he finds a phone."

Walter pulled carefully into one of the spaces along the back of the lot that were a little wider than the rest so that his car was sitting perfectly between the lines. Their friends were always teasing him about his perfect parking but she thought it was cute.

"Thanks for the ride, Beta Knapp"

He grinned, "Any time Honey."

"The guys are going to be so surprised."

"Yeah." He looked nervous.

"Come on. I want to see their faces when they realize." And make sure he got safely to his suite, but she didn't say that.

Amazingly, they didn't encounter a single member of the Wolfborne pack or any of Alpha Meyer's men while they walked to the dorm and up to his room. In fact, they only saw three people and that was from a distance.

Walter unlocked the door and pushed it open so she could enter first.

Luca glanced up from the couch when they walked in. "Oh good. You're back. I've been trying to figure out how to do this problem for the last hour. Can you help me out Honey?"

"Sure." She walked across the room to the TV and turned it off. Nathan had stopped with the snack bar he was eating half-way to his mouth and was sniffing the air when she turned around.

"What's going on?" he asked, looking toward Walter.

139

"Guys," Honey said, extending an arm toward Walter, "May I present Beta Knapp of the Nameless pack."

Nathan blinked. "What?"

Luca tossed his notebook to the side and stood. "What kind of cockamamie name is that?" He marched over to Walter's side and sniffed. "Zavier."

"Yep."

"He's the alpha," Honey said unnecessarily.

"How is that possible?" Nathan asked.

"Genetics," Walter shrugged. "That's why Alpha Meyer dislikes him so much. It's just temporary until he finds another pack."

"Walter did it to keep him sane," Honey added.

"Never thought one of us would be a beta," Nathan said, then grinned and clapped Walter on the shoulder. "Congratulations."

"Yeah, congratulations," Luca said, attacking his other shoulder.

"I'm going to change and get my books. You still have time to study chemistry with me Walter?" Honey asked.

"Yeah. I have a test too. I can work on my essay later."

She was half-way down the sidewalk between the boys' dorm and hers when she smelled them: Alpha Meyer's thugs. She whipped around to face them before they could touch her. "What do you want?"

"Where's Zavier?"

She heard the scuff of shoe behind her right before an arm went for her neck, but she was already ducking and spinning and punching and kicking. The last hit had her attacker rolling on the ground, cradling his knee. She only had a split second to verify he was down before she sensed movement from the two men now to her side. She attacked before they could, knocking the closest one off balance with a sweep, then springing up to to punch the third man hard in the side of the neck. He stumbled back a little and put up his hands.

"We just want to talk."

He was lying. "No you don't. Stay away from me and stay away from Zavier."

If she'd been alone and not able to freeze people, the smart thing to do would be to run, but she wasn't alone. The fight had garnered the attention of a couple of witches coming out of her dorm. She didn't know their names, but she'd seen them around. "Call campus security!" she yelled.

"Stay out of this. It's a wolf matter," the man on the ground shouted.

"Wolves are in charge of security," Honey reminded him.

The second man lunged at her, but she was ready. She squatted and used his momentum to flip his much larger body over her own, then landed on his face with an elbow. Something cracked and it wasn't her elbow. The man she'd hit in the neck decided to try again, but he was still clumsy from the hit on his vagus nerve. She rolled away from his attempted grab and into a spinning back-kick that knocked him right on top of his friend who was unsuccessfully trying to stop the blood that was flowing out of his nose.

"You all right, Honey?"

She glanced up at the young man who had appeared and was standing over the guy holding his knee. Rhys. She couldn't remember him ever talking directly to her before.

"Yeah."

"The pack is on the way."

She had a moment to wonder what he meant, then a whole flood of wolves poured out of the boys' dorm. Just down the road, a second flood came out of the fancy girls' dorm. The two groups flowed together in a big circle around them. Brayton pushed through to stand by her side. "What happened?"

"That's what I want to know," an older wolf wearing a campus security shirt said, stepping out of one of the amazingly fast golf carts the security people used around campus. He wasn't from her pack, but he wasn't from the Wolfborne pack either.

"They attacked me."

"Who else was with you?"

"It was just me."

He raised a doubtful eyebrow. "You took down three men by yourself?"

"Yes." He could smell she wasn't lying.

"Well, all right then." He sniffed. "They're Wolfborne and you're..."

"Mooney," Brayton supplied.

The security wolf sniffed at Honey again. "Okay, if you say so. We'll take it from here."

Three other security guards, each with their own cart, had parked behind the first. Brayton took her elbow and pulled her out of the circle while the guards surrounded the men.

"Are you okay?" he asked in a low voice once they were clear of the circle.

"Yes. I'm fine."

"Why did they attack you?"

142

"Zavier. Walter and I helped him escape the clinic this morning, right out from under their noses."

Brayton sniffed. "That's why you smell like him."

"I guess."

To her great surprise, he abruptly pulled her into a hug. She couldn't have hugged him back even if she wanted to though. He had her arms pinned to her sides.

"I'm glad you're safe." He kissed her forehead, right where all the alphas tended to kiss her, then let her go.

Wobbling from the release and overwhelming scent of his body spray, she said the first thing that popped into her head. "I'm...going to change now."

18

Honey

The problem with belonging to a pack of two, one of whose members was on the run, was that it was hard to know who to trust. They could somewhat hide the fact that Walter now belonged to a different pack simply by surrounding him with Little wolves, but that was hard to do in WOLF class where members from different packs were expected to mix. Case in point, Brayton and his friends showed up at the same time the guys did. Even though they were at least fifteen feet apart, she saw Brayton sniff the air and turn suddenly toward her friends. She leaped to her feet from where she was stretching and joined her friends just as Brayton reached them, still sniffing. He stopped right in front of Walter.

"You aren't in the Little Pack anymore."

Walter shook his head. Honey quickly and quietly made introductions. "Future alpha Brayton, meet Beta Walter."

"Beta?"

"Zavier is an alpha," Honey explained. "Walter joined his pack to keep him stable."

Brayton blinked. "Huh. I knew he was strong, but I didn't realize he was alpha strong."

"Stronger than his cousins. That's why their father doesn't like him," she said.

Brayton lifted a hand to grasp Walter's shoulder. "Congratulations. It takes a good man to leave his pack to help out another."

"Thanks."

Brayton dropped his hand to look around at the grounds now crawling with wolves. "I don't know what Alpha Meyer would do if he realized you belong to Zavier's pack, maybe nothing, but after yesterday I think it's better if he doesn't know."

"We agree," Nathan said. "Our whole pack is in on the S&P plan."

"S&P?" Honey asked.

"Surround and protect."

"I'll order my pack to help too," Brayton said.

"Why does it have to be an order?" She shook her head when they all looked at her like she was an alien. "Never mind. Do you know what happened to those guys who attacked me?"

"Released. They were under orders from their alpha, but because they attacked you on campus, Alpha Meyer is going to pay a hefty fine."

"He told them to attack me?"

"No. He told them to find Zavier and they decided to question you, but you were a little more resistant than they expected," Brayton snorted.

"Enough chatting over there!" Captain Young yelled. "Get your runs in unless you don't *want* to do the obstacle course. I have no problem making you run the whole time."

"Go," Honey ordered, giving Luca a push. The obstacle course was not something to miss.

Tuesday, right after classes were out, she rode back to the pack lands with Brayton and Cici for the Thanksgiving holiday. Honey was more than happy to let Cici sit in the front seat with Brayton.

She'd never been to a Thanksgiving celebration where she knew a lot of the people. She and Mom had always volunteered at a soup kitchen during the holidays because her dad couldn't be with them and there was no point doing all that cooking for just the two of them.

To wolves, the entire pack was family which meant they were all there. Rows and rows of tables were set up in the biggest barn on the pack lands. They didn't just have turkey, they had venison, duck, a whole pig, and three tables of desserts. Afterward there were games outside and in. Most of the younger people, herself included, played outside games like capture the flag and rugby. By the end of the day, she was thankful for her bed and that Brayton wasn't hogging the shower.

Unfortunately, she didn't get to stay in bed long. Luna Lynn woke her up to take her to the 'shopping Olympics' at a ridiculous time in the morning.

Honey was ready to quit Black Friday shopping as soon as they got to the mall and saw the people in line at the front door. Not Lynn. She smirked and led Honey and the at least ten other women with them to another entrance that hardly anyone knew about. Lynn then spent the next several hours trying to convince Honey to buy stuff, but she didn't, except for a pair of boots and a coat. Honey planned to make everyone cookies for Christmas and for that she only needed the ingredients. There was a kitchen on every floor in the dorm already stocked with basic cooking equipment.

Saturday night Alpha Brandon led the pack on a run even though the full moon wasn't until Monday. All she had to do was follow Lynn and Bernadette. It was easy. She didn't need to use a single one of Brayton's commando signals, and, for the first time, she really enjoyed herself.

Although the Little and Mooney pack lands weren't exactly close, Walter came on Sunday morning to take her to church, then back to college. There were a few other wolves who attended the small church, but none of them belonged to her pack, and they usually kept to themselves.

Monday morning, the temperature dropped below freezing just in time for WOLF class. It was so cold Greg was wearing a knit cap with a tractor on it instead of his signature green headband. She and Greg had finished their laps and started their exercises by the time Brayton and his gang appeared one minute before class started, as usual. She grinned and waved when he looked her way.

He actually, almost smiled and gave her a nod.

Captain Young jogged to a stop in front of everyone. "Okay kids, it's cold today, but hopefully you were all mature enough to dress for the weather. We have a guest today, Damien Meyer, future alpha of the Wolfborne pack. He's here to observe how well his pack members' training is coming along. He's also a two-time State MMA champion, so this should be an interesting class. Go run."

What was Damien doing here? Captain Young must not have heard what happened the week before. Should she tell him?

Oh no. Walter.

Honey immediately looked around for her friend. There he was – running with the rest of the guys and a few other members of the Little pack on the far side of the field. There was no way he heard Captain Young. Damien was…she scanned the field and the bleachers and finally stopped on a large truck parked in the lot. It was running and had been running for a while. The whole lot was filled with a blue haze from whatever was shooting out the exhaust. She couldn't see who was inside through the tinted windows, but she had a very strong suspicion. She finished her stretch and started doing high knees in the opposite direction than they usually ran so she could catch Walter before he got close. She met up with them just past the bleachers.

Walter immediately knew something was up. "What's wrong Honey?"

"Damien Meyer is here to observe the class."

"Ah."

"Don't worry, we've got this," Luca said. "You know what to do people," Luca said to everyone who was running with them. "S&P."

She ran another lap with them. Once everyone was done, Captain Young told them to split up into groups. She started to split off with the guys like she normally did but Cici grabbed her arm.

"No. Come with us."

"But I need to protect Walter."

"You're going to lead Damien right to him."

She glanced toward Damien through the corner of her eye. He'd finally stepped out of his warm truck and was standing next to Captain Young, but his eyes were on her.

"Okay."

Captain Young ordered them to pair up. Cici declared Honey was her partner. Honey placed herself so she could keep an eye on Damien who had started wandering through the pairs near the bleachers.

"I've been looking forward to this rematch for a long time."

"Rematch?" Honey repeated automatically, not taking her eyes off Damien.

"Yeah, remember, you beat me that first time right before Brayton broke your ribs. That was a fluke, by the way. I went easy on you."

"Mmm." Damien was talking to some of his own pack. They wouldn't know about Zavier, but they'd know who her friends were.

Cici shoved Honey hard enough that she fell down. She didn't get up. From the ground she could watch without distraction and she had to come up with a strategy to protect Walter in case the S&P didn't work.

Cici nudged her with a toe. "Get up."

When Honey didn't respond, Cici grabbed her arm and pulled her up. "Honey, look at me." Honey ignored her. Damien was looking around like he was trying decide who else to question. Cici shook Honey and pushed her in a circle until her back was to Damien. "Look at me!" Honey did so Cici would say whatever it was and get it over with.

"You want to keep his attention off your friends, then fight me. Really fight me. Nothing grabs the attention of a man like that than two chicks going after each other. Trust me."

"It won't last long enough though."

Cici pushed Honey away with a smirk. "Maybe not on your side." She glanced over Honey's shoulder. "He's looking this way. Now is our chance to get his attention."

Honey glanced over her shoulder and felt her feet disappear out from under her.

Cici grabbed her shirt and hauled her up. "Stupid. You should never take your eyes off your opponent."

"I was trying not to."

Cici shook her, then pushed her, hard, so that she fell again. "Me, you idiot. He's over there. I'm right here. Pay attention to me."

At this rate, if she did have to rush over to help Walter, Cici would probably tackle her and insist she fight past her first. Honey glanced over her shoulder again. Damien was standing next to a couple of guys from the Silvermane pack, but he was looking in their direction. Maybe Cici was right. Maybe a good fight would keep him distracted. At the least, if she took out Cici, she'd be free to help Walter.

Cici looked down on her with disgust as she started to get up. "You're pathetic."

"Problem girls?"

Cici turned to complain to Captain Young. Honey took advantage of Cici's distraction and her position on the ground to sweep Cici's legs out from under her.

"No problem Captain," she chimed, rolling to her feet before Cici could recover from her surprise fall. "Cici just needs to learn to keep her eyes on her opponent."

"Ugh, you twit."

Cici dove at her from the ground. Not wanting to get into a wrestling match, Honey did a diving roll over her and popped up on her feet.

"Stop grinning," Cici snarled, right before she launched herself at Honey again.

Cici had been practicing or she truly had been taking it easy on her before. Honey had been practicing too though, with wolves instead of humans. Cici was stronger than her, but Honey knew more moves thanks to all the different classes she'd taken. Cici landed a few hits, but neither of them were truly trying to take the other down, at least Honey wasn't. Cici was right about getting Damien's attention. He was so distracted by their fight, he wasn't bothering to observe anyone else any more.

Cici wasn't smiling but she wasn't frowning either. Based on the limited range of emotions Honey had seen her display, she was enjoying herself. Honey was too.

Abruptly, Cici's face changed. She looked meaner and harder and came at Honey like she wanted to hurt her instead of just practice. Cici aimed a kick at her head, which Honey ducked, then hit Cici in the ribs. Honey jumped back and came right back at her with a kick and a punch that knocked the bigger girl back a few feet. Cici wasn't done though. She came at Honey with fists flying like Honey had insulted her mother or something equally egregious. Honey took a few hits, then dove into a roll and delivered a Kyokushin wheel kick to Cici's face. Cici fell into the other students who had stopped to watch.

Honey bounced on the balls of her feet, waiting for Cici to spring up at her again. When she didn't, Honey stepped forward and offered her a hand.

"You all right?"

Cici wiggled her jaw. "What kind of a crazy move was that?"

"Karate."

"You have a black belt or something?"

"Yeah."

Cici rolled her eyes. "Of course you do."

"It looked cool, but you left yourself open for attack," Damien said with a voice just as oily smooth as his father's.

He stepped closer. The mix of exhaust from his truck and the abundance of cheap cologne he'd doused himself with was not pleasant, nor was the way he towered over her. It almost looked like he was using his alpha power, but there was no reason he should be.

"I could give you a few tips if you want."

"You know karate?"

He punched his palm with his fist. "I know wolf."

"Um, sure." If he was with her, he couldn't sniff out Walter.

His tips evolved into a lesson with her and different people from her pack as his models. He wasn't a bad teacher, she just didn't like the way he kept touching her to place her body in different poses. She did her best to keep her face blank though. After several minutes, and to her great relief, Captain Young told them to run two more miles then head back to the dorms. She bowed to Damien as she'd bowed to all her martial arts instructors, told him thank you, then turned to sprint away, but he caught her shoulder.

"What are you doing Friday night?"

Hopefully watching the rest of Luca's movie.

"Stuff. Why?"

He smirked. He probably thought he looked cool. He didn't. "Cancel. We're going on a date."

She pulled out of his grip. "No. You're a teacher and you're old."

He puffed up. "I said cancel."

"Fine, date's canceled. Let's never mention it again." She ran and buried herself in the center of the fast group, which did not include the Little wolves. Damien planted himself by the entrance near the bleachers and followed her around with his eyes. It was creepy. At the end of her last lap, she veered off and went over the fence on the other side of the bleachers where he couldn't see her and took off toward her dorm. She was congratulating herself on avoiding him when she realized she should have let him talk to her so Walter could slip by unnoticed. She slowed and turned back, but there was already a lone, tall, skinny form loping after her.

She was so relieved to see him, she met him with a huge hug. "Walter!"

He squeezed her back. "Honey. Good idea with the fence."

She looked back. She could still see the bleachers. "Think he's figured it out yet?"

"Let's not found out."

19

Brayton

A familiar figure broke from the pack of over-achievers in front of them and basically jumped over the chain-length fence. She would have cleared it completely if she hadn't kicked off the top with one of her feet.

"What's she up to now?"

"Avoiding Damien I bet," Cici said beside him.

"Avoiding him? They looked pretty chummy during class." Honey had let Damien touch her. In fact, there had been no sign of her perverse nature while he posed her like a mannequin for his impromptu lesson.

Cici shook her head. "She was only putting up with him to keep him away from Walter. Look."

Another figure in front of them scaled the fence. Walter chose to grab the top of the fence and swing his long legs over instead of jumping it like Honey.

"You know, if she didn't drive you crazy, she'd make a good beta," Cici said.

"What!?" Malcolm and Brayton said together.

"She can't hear," Malcolm said.

"Only in wolf form," Cici said dismissively, "and she more than makes up for that with her speed and fighting skills as a human. She's smart and she's loyal, maybe not to our pack yet but she is to her friends, and she's immune to alpha powers. Brayton, all of us appreciate what you've done by choosing us, but none of us can resist alpha powers the way Honey can. Most alphas have at least one beta who can."

"She has no respect for authority."

"That's not true. She respects her teachers. She respects your mom. It's only alphas she seems to have trouble with."

"Don't you think that would be a serious issue when it comes to pack politics?"

Cici shrugged. "She's new to pack life. With a little training, she'll figure it out."

"Are you sure you're all right?" Malcolm asked. "She did nail you pretty hard."

Cici rubbed her jaw. "I'm fine."

"That was a cool move she used on you," Rhys dared to say. "You were going at her pretty hard. I thought she was going down."

"That wasn't me. Jerk-face Damien was pushing me with his power."

"He was!" Brayton exclaimed. He'd sensed Damien was using his power but he hadn't realized why. He should have.

Cici grabbed Brayton's arm. "Let it go. It's his word against mine. There's nothing you can do about it now."

"I can confront him."

"He'll deny it."

Brayton didn't argue. She was wrong to tell him not to confront Damien. Protecting the pack was his job. There was no point in being an alpha if he couldn't.

They finished their run in front of the bleachers. Damien was still standing by the entrance to the field searching every face that went by. Brayton called up as much of his power as he could and stomped over to him. He didn't accuse or ask Damien what had happened. He simply told him how it was going to be.

"You are not to use your power on members of my pack."

Damien crossed his arms over his wide chest and stared down at him. "You think you're alpha enough to make me?"

"I don't think, I know."

It was the first time he'd had a true stand-off against another alpha. Damien's power hammered his, his face turning redder and redder. He looked constipated. Brayton might have too, but he didn't let up even after he'd forced Damien to lower his head and he'd felt the man's power fade. Brayton kept pushing until Damien turned and walked toward his decked-out show-pony of a truck and climbed into the cab.

Brayton turned around to find Captain Young right behind him. "Mr. Mooney, is there some reason you decided to use your alpha power against a guest instructor? If so, I hope it's a good one, because otherwise you're out of the class."

Unlike when he'd clawed a certain girl with a kitten, Brayton didn't feel worried or upset. He'd done what he had to do and if that meant failing the class, then he would. Dad would understand. "He used his power on

Cici. My dad told Damien and his brother and Alpha Meyer to leave our pack alone. It's my job to enforce my dad's commands. If that means I'm out of the class, so be it."

Captain Young gave a quick nod. "I'll be in contact with your dad then. If you don't hear from me otherwise, you can come to class on Wednesday."

"Yes, Sir."

Cici waited exactly three steps before she punched him. "Why didn't you listen?"

"You are part my of pack. It's my job to protect you. Now he knows he can't just use the people in our pack for his own purposes. That's important Cici. It's not something I could let go."

Predictably, two hours later, in the middle of class, he got a text from his mom. He called her as soon as the class was over because she'd complain if he didn't and so he could get it over with.

"Hey Mom."

"Hey Brayton, have you seen Honey lately? She's not answering her phone."

That's why she texted him? He should have been relieved. Instead it made him irritated. "Uh, yeah. She's fine. She's probably in class. The little idiot turns her phone completely off when she's in class."

"Ah, so she won't be distracted. Smart child. That's probably part of the reason she's top in all her classes. Maybe you should try it."

His phone made a cracking noise and he abruptly realized how tight he was holding it. "If I did, you wouldn't be getting a phone call from me right now."

157

"True. Well anyway, if you see her, can you tell her to call me? I'm getting the menu together for her birthday and I want to make sure I serve something she likes."

"Mom she's not picky. She eats the same food as everyone else."

"I know, but I wanted to ask in case there's something special she would like. Remember when you insisted I serve sardines?"

"I was eight. It was a phase. She's going to be eighteen."

"Eighteen-year-olds can have phases too. Oh, I've got to go. Don't forget to tell her Brayton. Love you."

"Mom…"

She hung up before he could tell her about Damien. That would probably come back to bite him. He turned his phone off before dropping it into his backpack. He had a class after all, and he could do without distractions, apparently.

20

Honey

Ever since Alpha Day Honey had wanted to go to the library and see if she could find her mom in the yearbooks, if they existed, but with Thanksgiving and all the tests the teachers had thrown at them right before the holiday, she hadn't had a chance. Monday after classes, she finally had an hour. She marched herself through the cold to the grandest-looking building on campus, at least on the outside. Inside was, eh. The tired-looking librarian on the first floor directed Honey to the top floor. Honey dutifully climbed the stairs expecting another large room with low ceilings and bookshelves that blocked the sunlight from the windows. She stepped out of the stairwell and her mouth dropped open. The vaulted ceilings and tall windows made the space feel huge, like a cathedral, yet an abundance of cushy, comfortable chairs interspersed with the occasional wooden table promised the perfect place to study. There were even window seats! She loved window seats. A row of bookshelves jutted into the room from the north wall, but the room was so large, they were almost unnoticeable.

She found her birth year and pulled that yearbook and the one before it off the shelf, then claimed a window seat. The lawn where the witch's craft fair had been stretched out like a green and yellow carpet beneath her. For a moment, she imagined she was a princess looking over her palatial estate and that the students walking past on the sidewalk in their present-day winter clothes were mere peasants. Did the guys know about this floor? She'd have to bring them. They could be knights or something.

Turning her attention to the books in her lap, she opened the newer one first. She'd never looked at a yearbook before. She had no idea the college had so many clubs and sports. Not all the pictures had names under them and some shots only showed people from very far away. She was wondering if she should come back with a magnifying glass when she discovered there were pages with rows and rows of individual photos and names in the back of the book. She scanned every face under the seniors' pages. Her mom wasn't there. She found Alpha Silver though. He was one of the most handsome guys on the page. Her dad's picture was in the Sophomore pages. His face was slimmer and his hair a little longer, but the way his eyes lit up when he smiled was the same. Her heart trembled thinking about him. She was very tempted to take a picture of the picture with her phone, but she knew better. Pictures were dangerous. Mom hadn't kept any pictures of dad or her where people could find them so no one would be able to tie them together. The strategy had worked. Her mom was gone but, as far as she knew, whoever had killed her mom didn't know about her.

Honey shut the book before her tears could damage the pages.

Her mom wasn't in the second book, nor was her dad. That didn't make sense. How could her dad be a sophomore without becoming a freshman first? Was it possible he just didn't get into the book? What happened if someone didn't send in a picture or show up to get their picture taken? The guys would probably know.

On her way back to get what would have been her mom's freshman and sophomore years, she saw a girl walking very purposely toward the back corner of the library past the bookcases. Thinking there might be a fancy hidden study area, Honey grabbed the books she wanted and followed her.

It wasn't fancy. It wasn't even enticing. None of the sunlight pouring in through the windows on the other side of the room reached the back corner. There were a few lumpy-looking chairs, a couch big enough to sleep on that looked like it had been there since the seventies, and a table with an even older lamp. That was it. Even the girl wasn't there. Honey turned to go but the faint scents of stainless steel, cotton, and magic made her halt in her tracks.

She spun back around. She'd smelled that odd combination before near the restricted section of the craft fair. Why was there a shielding spell here? What could it be hiding?

She followed her nose to the very back corner behind the furniture. It looked like a blank section of wall, but the way the hair on her arms was standing and tingling indicated otherwise.

The smart thing to do was walk away but, she looked over her shoulders just to be sure, for once she was alone and free to be a witch. Besides, other than the tingling, there was no indication of danger. It was just magic.

She lifted her hand toward the wall. The tingling grew stronger the closer her fingers got to the surface until it felt like she'd dipped her hand into a well of static, but it didn't shock her. The shock didn't happen until she made contact. Blue sparks shot from her hand and across the surface of the wall like crooked spokes of a wheel but instead of ending in a circle, they ended on the outline of a door-sized rectangle. Even after she pulled her hand away, the blue kept going, flowing together until it formed a complete rectangle. The wall inside the rectangle sank into the plaster and became an old-fashioned, plain, white wooden door that looked like the door to a storage closet.

She expected the door to be locked since someone had used magic to shield it, but to her surprise, the knob turned easily. Cautiously, because that seemed like the prudent thing to be when opening an unknown magical door, she opened it a few inches. When nothing jumped out at her, she peeked around the edge.

The room beyond was *not* a closet.

The lingering auras of hundreds of witches and the scents of thousands of spells poured over her. It was like walking into a scented candle store with all the candles lit. For a moment, she was so overwhelmed she couldn't move. In desperation, she used a little of her own magic to pull air from her side of the door to line her nasal passages with a thin layer of less-smelly air. When she could breath, she opened the door further and took a look around at the second library. Second because it was nothing like the

162

library she was currently standing in. This one looked like something from the 1800s instead of the mishmash of modern in the rest of the library building. She stepped through the door onto a metal balcony that went all the way around a long, narrow room. Beneath her were more balconies, each making a complete circle around the room and connected only by narrow metal steps. Ancient-looking electric lamps hung randomly from the bottom of each balcony, leaving circles of yellow light and highlighting even older-looking books crammed onto wooden bookshelves that formed every wall. At either end of the narrow room, the balconies widened to form small seating areas with either cushy chairs or wooden tables with chairs.

She stepped forward to the railing and looked down. She'd never had a problem with heights, but the sheer number of balconies and the narrowness of the room made her feel like she was about to fall forward even though she had a tight grip on the railing.

The room didn't descend forever. It probably went no deeper than the level of the ground outside or perhaps a bit below. The very bottom floor had a table at one end and a few rows of chairs facing it, like a classroom. Maybe that's what it was.

"How did you get in here?"

Honey jumped high enough to fly over the railing, at least it felt like it. Clutching her chest, she turned to face the owner of the shrill voice. The woman was younger than she expected, perhaps her mom's age, and looked exactly like you'd imagine a professional librarian would look, or actually, exactly like the librarian in the Mummy movie, except a little older and not as cute and probably a little taller.

Honey pointed behind her. "Through the door."

The librarian squinted at her and leaned closer as if that would help her detect if she was lying. Who knew, maybe it would. "You could see the door?"

"Yes."

"You just walked to the corner and saw the door?" the librarian challenged.

"No. I smelled magic and followed it and touched the wall and then I saw the door."

"And it just showed up?"

"No, it shocked me first."

The woman straightened and frowned at the door. "Huh."

"Where am I?"

"The library, although not in an area you should be."

"This is the witch's library, isn't it?"

The librarian's gaze sharpened again. "You've heard of it?"

"No. It just makes sense. You can't keep books on magic where the humans can find them, but this is a place of learning and witches need books on magic, ergo," Honey waved her hand around, "secret library."

"Ergo. Wow, I don't think I've ever heard someone of your generation use that word."

"People tell me I'm different."

"Mmm." She nodded at Honey's hand. "What have you got there?"

"Oh." Honey lifted the yearbooks up so the librarian could see she hadn't taken anything from her shelves, "I was looking for my…people I know."

"Well, the lighting is much better out there." The librarian waved at the door. "Why don't you go back to what you were doing. Just forget everything you saw here."

The tone of her voice and the scent of mothballs clued Honey into what the woman was attempting. She instinctively took a step back and shook her head although she didn't think you could shake off a forgetfulness spell. "Can I look around first?"

"Why? You're a wolf. I didn't think wolves wanted anything to do with magic."

"I like magic."

"Really?" The librarian's tone dripped with disbelief. "Let me guess, you think if you know how witches cast their spells you'll be able to somehow stop them or use it against them."

"No, although I do have a friend who was cursed. Do you have anything on breaking curses?"

"Cursed?"

Honey pretended she didn't hear the doubt in the librarian's voice. "Yes. Did you hear about the wolf who tried to kill all those people at the club several weeks ago? He wasn't crazy. He was cursed. One of the waitresses put a potion in his drinks so she could control him, but it also made him depressed. He tried to commit suicide twice. The witch's council said there was no cure. I don't believe that."

"How is he now?"

"Better, but I'd feel more comfortable about it if I knew more about curses."

"I doubt that, but I do have book you can look through. There's a catch though."

"What?"

"If I don't erase your memory, I have to put a binding spell on you. You won't be able to tell anyone about this place. Which means if you try to speak or write or even hint at its existence, you won't be able to."

Honey didn't like the idea of being bound, but she really didn't like the idea of having her memory messed with. "Will my mouth stop moving or will I get knocked unconscious?"

The librarian blinked. "Your mouth will still move, you just won't be able to make words."

"For how long?"

"As long as you're trying to say anything about the library."

"Have you performed this spell on anyone else?"

"Only every witch that comes through the college."

Did that mean her mom had been bound? That would explain why she never told her about this place, which brought up another question. "If you bind everyone, how does anyone know the library is here?"

"You ask a lot of questions."

"Yep. Best way to find things out, other than reading."

The librarian gave a little huff. "If you feel that someone would benefit from using the library, you will still be able to direct them to the main library and tell them to ask for Mrs. Withers, although wolves aren't allowed, so don't bother."

"Will you allow me to come back?"

"I won't ban you unless you do something to warrant it, if that's what you're asking, but the library has wards to prevent others and wolves and witches with ill intent from entering. I don't know why the wards let you through this time. They might be glitching, in which case you may not be able to get in again after I refresh them.

"Bind me. I want to remember even if it's the only time I can come."

The librarian made a fist and tapped the large, gaudy ring she wore on Honey's forehead. "You are bound."

"That's it?"

The librarian shrugged. "It's a lot easier than saying the whole spell every time. Come along. The book you want is down a level. You can't check it out and trying to take books out of the library without my permission will automatically get you banned. She looked back over her shoulder and wiggled her eyebrows. "There's a spell for that."

21

Brayton

He was exhausted. He knew using alpha power could take a toll, but he'd never used so much that he actually felt it. All he wanted to do was crash, but his stomach was demanding he fill it first. He usually waited for Malcolm and Rhys because it was polite, not because they were like a gaggle of girls that had to do everything together like Cici teased. Tonight, though, he was so hungry he went by himself. They'd catch up.

He'd just taken his first bite when he felt Damien enter the room. Technically, announcing his presence by leaking a bit of alpha power wouldn't hurt anyone in Brayton's pack, but it was still irritating. Was Damien doing it to get a rise out of him? Brayton leaned forward to take a bite and looked out of the corner of his eye toward the source of the power at the same time. Great, Damien was coming his way.

"Brayton. We meet again."

Without asking, the alpha-to-be pulled out a chair and plopped down at the table. "You have good taste. This is the same table where my brother and I used to sit when we were here. I used to sit in the exact same spot you're sitting now."

Brayton made a note to grab a new chair from across the room next time he was in the cafeteria, and to bring some wipes.

A boy from Damien's pack slid a loaded tray in front of him. A girl added a drink. Another girl flipped open a large paper napkin and spread it on his lap. A third put a small vase with a rose in front of him. Damien didn't even look at them. The four melted back into the cafeteria crowd as soon as they were done. It was surreal.

Damien picked up the rose and sniffed it, then shook his head and put it back. "I've heard that old roses, those that haven't been domesticated, have a much more potent smell."

"Why are you here?"

He shrugged and leaned back to look around like he owned the place. "Just visiting." He let out a long sigh. "This place brings back a lot of memories."

He'd only graduated maybe two years ago yet he was acting like it had been twenty. Brayton didn't point that out. The less talking the better. Unfortunately, he couldn't leave while Damien was there. He had to protect his pack.

"I'm surprised you're here all alone. Where's your girlfriend?"

"Girlfriend?"

"Maybe that's the wrong word. Intended? No. Object of your interest. Yeah, that's it. I hate to say this, but I don't think she returns your interest."

Brayton gave him a 'what the hell are you talking about' look and turned his attention back to his food.

169

Whatever game Damien was trying to play, he wasn't interested.

"What, did I hit a sore spot? She not receptive to your overtures?"

Receptive to his overtures? Where had Damien come up with that phrase? He sounded like a Victorian novel or like a character in those shows Brayton's mom liked to watch occasionally.

"Actually," Damien tilted the chair back and looked around again. "I'm rather surprised you're here all alone. You were alone at the picnic too, except for your mom. I didn't realize you were a loser, I mean, loner."

Brayton wished at that moment he had the power to knock over chairs with a thought. Damien, irritatingly, stayed upright.

"Hey Brayton." Cici slid her tray onto the table beside him. "Having a meeting without me?"

He grinned at her like she was the only woman in his life. "You know I wouldn't do that."

She played along, returning the grin with a side of sultry. Even though he knew she didn't mean it, it did something to his insides.

She looked around like she was truly curious. "Where are the guys?"

"They're coming. They wanted to drop their stuff at the dorm."

She gazed at him with a look that could have melted butter if he had any. "Hmm. I guess that means I have you all to myself." She pushed her chair closer to his so that their legs were nearly touching, then reached onto his tray and swiped his soda.

"Hey!" He protested with mock anger.

170

She put the straw to her lips and took a sip then gave it back to him with a shrug. "I just wanted to make sure it was worthy of you."

"Uh-huh."

Damien's eyes flicked between the two of them suspiciously. "How's your jaw?" he asked Cici.

"Fine. I think the hit looked worse than it was."

"Do you and that girl, what's her name, Honey, practice together often?"

Cici laughed.

"She's pretty good."

Cici shrugged.

"So how long have you two been together?" Damien waved his finger between Brayton and Cici.

Cici grinned and looked at Brayton as if he were her everything. "When have we not been together? Didn't we have a play date when we were like a month old?"

He shook his head. "I can't remember that far back."

She slugged him playfully. "I can't believe you've forgotten our first date."

He grabbed her hand. "I'd never forget that." He meant it. They'd both been fifteen. He took her to the movies. Afterward, he took her home and kissed her behind the tree in front of her house. It was like kissing his mom. They'd decided to just be friends after that.

She gave him another one of those sultry grins. If Cici ever found the man she was waiting for, he was going to be one lucky guy.

"Sorry about earlier," Damien said suddenly. "I didn't realize she was yours," he nodded toward Cici. "I just wanted to see how good the little rogue actually was."

Brayton wasn't sure what to say. He hadn't expected an apology. What was Damien playing at?

"Did you know she was a good fighter when you picked her up or that she was smart?"

"No."

"You found her at a homeless shelter?"

Mom had told everyone as much, so he nodded.

"Have you found any others like her?"

"No."

"You got lucky then."

"I guess." Had he? He hadn't thought about it before. College would have been a lot different without Honey. He probably wouldn't be so irritated all the time and he wouldn't have gotten demoted from leading the pack, but he might very well be in prison or in the hospital.

"You know anything about her parents?" Damien asked.

"Only what she's told me," which was true enough that Damien shouldn't detect a lie. "She doesn't know much herself. I don't think they even told her their real names."

"You think she was kidnapped?"

"I…I don't know." He'd never thought of that. That was about as feasible as the love-child idea especially since they'd discovered her dad *wasn't* married to another woman, although with him, it didn't rule out an angry girlfriend or two.

"Why would someone do that?" Cici asked. "I mean, she's nothing special."

"Isn't she though," Damien asked. His voice was both suggestive and suspicious. What was going on in his head? Wait, was that what his initial conversation was about? Did

172

he think Brayton had a thing for Honey? And why was he asking so much about her? Right, she'd frozen him and his brother. Knowing Damien, he probably wanted some of whatever spell Honey had used for himself.

"Well, she's got book smarts, I'll give her that," Cici conceded. "She's never mentioned being taken, so she had to have been taken very young if she was taken. No one would have been able to tell how smart she was when she was a baby."

"Maybe her mom couldn't have a child of her own and took her because the opportunity presented itself," Damien suggested.

"Maybe," Brayton agreed to keep him talking. He doubted it though. No one would do that and then spend the rest of their life living in isolation, would they? It didn't explain why Mathias Silver was involved either.

The meal went on forever. Damien stayed at the table, chatting with people when they came by and accepting plates of desserts from his pack like he was a mafia lord. Brayton didn't feel comfortable going back to his room and leaving his pack unguarded. After two hours, Damien finally got up. He left his tray on the table. Brayton and Rhys bussed theirs. Cici and Malcolm had long since gone to work on homework. Damien still didn't leave. He had to make one last pass at the tables where the members of his own pack sat. They seemed happy enough to see him, which was good, Brayton guessed. Brayton followed him outside.

"Are you coming back for Wednesday training?" He asked, pretending it was just to make conversation. They both knew it wasn't.

"No, little alpha. Your pack is safe. I'm getting too old to get up that early."

"Excellent."

Damien snorted. "You know, if you weren't such a mama's boy, we might be good friends."

He'd probably have to deal with the man for the rest of his life so instead of out-right denying that would ever happen, Brayton shrugged. "Stranger things have happened."

22

Honey

The book the librarian gave Honey was a small hardback with a plain red cover titled '*So You Think You've Been Cursed*'. Despite the informal name, it was very informative. Since she couldn't check it out and she might never be able to come back, Honey read the whole thing. She learned that anyone with powers could curse someone, even unintentionally, but unintentional curses were a lot easier to break. Depending on the skill of the caster and how much attention they paid to ensuring obvious avenues to break it were blocked, intentional curses could last for years or even beyond lifetimes. The only sure way to remove an intentional curse was to have the caster remove it. Alternately, a curse breaker might be able to remove it. Curse breakers were very rare, however, perhaps even extinct.

She wondered if she'd ever cursed her mom unintentionally. She didn't think so. She couldn't remember ever getting as mad as the book described.

Several hours past when she meant to leave the library, she exited back out the door under the close supervision of Mrs. Withers, if that was her name. The door didn't immediately disappear, but when she looked back after she reached the bookshelves, it was gone.

She'd planned to sit down and finally look at the yearbooks, but her phone started dinging and buzzing like everyone in the world was suddenly trying to reach her. She pulled it out of her backpack to see twenty messages and they were still coming. She clicked on the first one and her phone rang. Brayton? Why was he calling her?

"Hello?"

"Honey! Where have you been?"

"In the library."

"I've been trying to reach you for hours. Your friends are in panic mode. Let me guess, you had your phone off again."

"No. It was on."

"Why didn't you answer then?"

"I guess I wasn't getting any signal. I just walked into another room and all the messages started coming."

"Do you know what time it is?"

"Um," she pulled the phone away and looked down, "eight."

"Yes, eight. You didn't show up for dinner and everyone is worried because of Alpha Meyer. How could you be so inconsiderate?"

"I didn't realize what time it was."

"What could you have possibly been doing for so long?"

"Reading. I'm sorry. I truly didn't realize what time it was, and it was a once-in-a-lifetime opportunity. I'm leaving right now."

"Just stay there. I'll come and get you."

"You don't need to. I'll call my friends."

"I'm coming. Meet me at the front entrance."

Great, she got to walk with an angry Brayton. She sent a group text to the guys telling them that she was fine and that Brayton was coming to escort her from the library. After putting the yearbooks away, she ran down the three flights of stairs so Brayton couldn't grump at her for making him wait and because she was hungry. The faster they got back to the dorm, the faster she could eat.

23

Brayton

He was half-afraid he'd have to scour the library looking for her, but Honey was there, right where he'd asked her to be, at the top of the steps leaning on the interior wall of the entryway.

She pushed off the wall and smiled when she saw him, then thanked him for coming to get her. Did she not realize the seriousness of the situation or was she trying to soften him up so he wouldn't scold her? It wasn't going to work. It was her fault he wasn't currently snoozing in his warm bed.

He pointed to the sidewalk beside him. "Get down here, let's go."

Her smile evaporated with a sigh but she obediently jogged down the steps. She was obeying him. He should be pleased, but it irked him even more.

"You have got to..." an awful gemish of smells hit him when she reached the sidewalk. The strongest was the ozone-like smell of magic, but underneath was all the things he associated with magic: herbs, smoke, strong chemicals, books. He stepped back and waved his hand under his nose to clear the air. "What on earth have you been doing?"

"Reading."

"In what, a cauldron?"

"No." She turned away, but not fast enough for him to miss the corner of her mouth tilting up.

He wanted to shake her, but at the same time he didn't want to touch her. "Honey."

She turned to him and her smile so bright he swore it was giving off light. "I discovered something amazing – really, really cool. I probably won't ever get to see it again, but I am going to keep the memory as long as I can. I'm sorry for worrying everyone. I really am. Can you just forgive me and move on?"

"No."

Her sigh when she turned away made him feel guilty, which made him madder. "Honey, you don't…"

She grabbed the straps of her backpack and started running.

"Stop. I said STOP!"

She didn't even slow down and he remembered, belatedly, that using his alpha power on her was useless. He should just let her go. Of course if something happened to her, it would be all his fault, darn her. He started jogging after her.

His adrenaline kicked in when four figures materialized out of the dark and surrounded her. He prepared to release a surge of power, then saw one of them hug her – Luca based on his height and scrawniness. Luca waved his hand in front of his nose. Predictably, Honey punched him, then hugged him back.

179

She was giving another lame apology when Brayton got close enough to hear.

"I'm so sorry I made you guys worry about me. I didn't realize my phone wasn't working."

Luca patted her on the back. His desperation for her was embarrassing. "It's okay, Honey. Just don't do that again. Send us a text if you're going to do something unplanned."

"I'll try."

They turned their backs on him and started walking back to the dorm. That was it? They weren't going to berate her any further or bother to thank him? The whole lot of them was rude.

"What were you doing?" Walter asked.

Brayton stepped closer so he could hear better in case she told them more than she'd told him.

"Reading."

"What, a book on magic?" her blond friend asked.

"Kind of. It was a book on curses. I was trying to understand how they work. Did you know that anyone with magic can curse someone, and it happens a lot on accident? The moral: if you date a witch, don't make her mad. I wonder if wolves can do it too."

Blond boy laughed. "That would be a disaster. Can you imagine with the tempers some of the girls have?"

"I think our ability to sprout claws has probably made that feature evolutionarily defunct," Walter spouted.

"Where did you get the book?" her dark-skinned friend asked. His tone was oddly accusatory.

"From a librarian," Honey said cheerfully, way too cheerfully.

180

"They have books on magic in the library?" Luca asked.

"Why wouldn't they? At least a quarter of the students are witches."

Classic evasion tactic. She was hiding something.

"Where?"

"On the shelves."

"What shelves?"

Ha! Liam – that was his name – knew something was up too.

"The ones in the library."

"Where in the library?" Liam persisted.

"You'll have to find them yourself. Guys, I am starving. You want to split a pizza with me?"

"Sure, but can you change your clothes first?" Luca said.

"No. You cannot let her change the subject like that." Brayton stepped forward and planted himself in front of Honey. The magic emanating off her was still bad, but he could smell that intoxicating scent that was unique to her underneath. "Where in the library, Honey?"

She mumbled something under her breath.

"What was that?"

She turned her stubborn face up to him with her green eyes sparkling and he wanted to…nope. The fumes must be getting to him.

"Why are you so curious? Do you want to read books on magic?"

"No," he stepped closer, "but I would like to know why a member of my pack who was missing for hours now reeks of magic."

"I already told you. I was reading. Nothing bad happened. It was good, actually."

"Where in the library?"

"I can't tell you."

"Tell me."

"I can see you puffing up Brayton. You know that doesn't work on me."

It felt like he was shrinking when he turned off his power. Damn that girl. Now he was going to imagine he inflated like a big human-shaped balloon every time he used it.

"Why can't you tell him," Walter asked.

"A promise."

She was lying. He didn't need his sense of smell to tell him that.

"To whom?" he demanded.

"The librarian who gave me the book."

"Is this something to do with witches?" blond boy asked.

Honey nodded.

"A secret?"

She nodded again.

"How did you find it?"

"It was an accident. The librarian said she was going to…change the locks after I left. That's why I couldn't leave until I finished the book."

"And I bet the presence of all that magic messed up your phone reception," Walter nodded.

"Magic? There wasn't any…"

"Honey, you reek," Walter said calmly. "There may not have been any while you were there, but there was definitely some at some point. Now why don't we go back to our respective dorms. You take a shower and we'll order pizza. We can stuff our faces while we watch Jeopardy."

She rewarded him with a grin that made Brayton want to growl. "You are the best Walter."

"I fully expect an amazing Christmas gift, or at least a good stash of Christmas cookies for my effort. Snickerdoodles are my favorite."

Luca waved his hands in a cancel motion. "No, no, no. Not snickerdoodle. Chocolate chip. Everyone loves chocolate chip."

The way Walter stared down his nose at Luca reminded Brayton of a tall, stately dog looking down at a yipping pup. "You love chocolate chip. If she gives me chocolate chip I'll be lucky to get *one*."

"Peanut butter," the blond said. "Classic."

Liam shook his head. "Have none of you ever had Christmas cookies before? They are supposed to be decorated. Sugar cookies. Now those are classic."

Honey stepped around Brayton like he was nothing more than a tree and they all walked away without another word to him, still bantering over cookies. Worse, they'd forgotten the most important flavor of Christmas cookie. He gave them several seconds to bring it up, but no. Honey's friends were dumb as rocks.

"Gingerbread! What's wrong with your pack? Everyone knows gingerbread is *the* Christmas cookie."

24

Honey

Wednesday morning was even colder than Monday. Honey donned her new coat and pulled the crocheted hat Lynn had given her as an early birthday present down as far as she could to cover her ears. She and Mom had never run in temperatures so low, but it wasn't bad. Once she did a couple of laps around the field and started to warm up, it was nice running in the crisp air. Sadly, the warmth did not survive the freezing metal bleachers Captain Young made them sit on for an announcement.

He cleared his throat and scanned them in their assortment of winter wear with a serious face, then snorted. "You guys look like you raided the homeless bin. Are those socks on your hands Mitchell?" He shook his head. "The schedule for The Games has finally been posted. We'll have the intra-collegiate tourney the last week in January. The winners will go on to the state tourney in February. Nationals are in March."

"What's he talking about?" Honey whispered to Luca.

"For those of you who have no idea what I'm talking about," Captain Young's eyes flicked briefly to her, "The Games are like wolf Olympics except they happen every year between the different colleges and don't include nearly as many sports. We generally field competitors in track, basketball, rugby, soccer, mixed martial arts, obstacle athletics, and swimming. You are all freshman, so it is unlikely that you will be chosen, but you still get to compete in the initial round this year so next year you'll know what to expect."

He pointed to her raised hand. "Question Honey?"

"What is obstacle athletics?"

"An obstacle course, but more challenging than what we have here. Think American Ninja Warrior. You need a lot of upper arm strength and control to finish it, which I can say with absolute certainty, no one in this class has. I've got sophomores who've been practicing since last year. They might – might have a chance to make it to state."

She'd seen American Ninja Warrior once in a hotel. It had looked like fun. She could do it. She just needed to work on her arm strength. They had a whole month and a long break from school. It wouldn't hurt to try.

"If you're interested in trying out for a team event, come see me before you leave. All of you will compete in the track and martial arts events. We will be practicing track events for the next two weeks and I expect you to practice over Christmas break so you're ready in January. We won't have class during finals week, but the field will be open if you need to let off steam. Yes, Honey?"

"What if you want to try out for obstacle athletics?"

185

"In January, I'll give the people with the top ten times on our obstacle course the option to compete against the upper classmen if they wish."

Perfect. She currently had the best time in the class. Unless a lot of people improved over Christmas break, she should be a shoo-in.

"If there are no other questions, class is dismissed."

Luca and Nathan popped up and headed toward Captain Young. She wasn't surprised Brayton, Cici, Rhys, and Malcolm went to see Captain Young too. She'd watched them play rugby on Thanksgiving break with the other wolves in the pack. She didn't know much about the sport, but they'd won by a lot.

"What are Luca and Nathan signing up for?" She asked Walter. She didn't know they played a sport. She felt bad. As their friend, she should have known.

"Soccer."

"Are you going to sign up for anything?"

"Basketball, but not until the crowd thins out." He tapped his forehead in the vacinity of Zavier's mark.

"How will you play then?"

He shrugged. "Maybe it won't be an issue by then." Walter looked around, then leaned closer. "He called me."

"How is he?"

"No headaches. An alpha offered him a job, but the alpha wanted to make sure Zavier was a good fit before accepting him into the pack."

"Makes sense. Did he tell you where?"

"No. I told him not to tell me."

"Good idea. How was your family?"

His family knew what he'd done, but Thanksgiving had been the first time he'd seen them since he became a beta.

"Fine. Mom got all teary-eyed, but Dad said he was proud of me. I think my older brothers were jealous."

"Of what?"

He tapped his chest with one finger. "Beta. No one in my family has ever been beta."

She looked down the bench where Liam was still chatting with Charlize. "Does Liam play any team sports?"

"He specialized in hurdles and long jump in high school. I'm sure he'll try out for that."

25

Honey

When Damien wasn't at training on Wednesday, Honey figured that was the last she'd see of him. She was wrong. Thursday, she stepped out of the building where she took one of her lab classes and suddenly Damien was right in front of her. Stupid wind was blowing the wrong way.

He smiled. Some girls would have found him handsome and maybe even charming. She did not.

"You're a hard wolf to find," he slimed.

"Not hard enough."

He chuckled. The deep, throaty sound set her nerves on edge. "I like a woman who plays hard to get."

"I'm sure you do."

She stepped around him. He didn't stop her. Nope, he turned and started walking beside her – upwind. After just a few steps, the cloying sent of his cologne was making it hard to breath. She took the sidewalk toward the library and into the breeze so she could breathe again.

"Where are we going?" he asked after they'd taken ten steps or so.

She couldn't exactly say 'the low-hanging tree over the picnic bench near the library so I can freeze you without anyone seeing'. Instead, she enacted a hastily concocted plan B which wasn't really a plan at all. She stopped and turned to him. They were blocking the sidewalk but there was plenty of room to go around and lots of witnesses in case things went south. "*We* aren't going anywhere. Not to be rude, but I have things to do and none of them involve you."

He stepped closer. She did not resist the urge to step back. She took a large step off the sidewalk and into the grass and put her hand up. "Please don't come any closer. Whatever cologne you are wearing is – I think I'm allergic to it."

He stopped and looked somewhat surprised for a moment, then a smarmy look appeared on his features and he stepped closer. "I'm not wearing cologne. You know what this means don't you?"

"You are really bad at choosing soap?"

He inhaled the air over her head like he was sniffing flowers. "The more I learn about you, the more intrigued I am."

She took another step back, causing a random human to change course. "Please don't be intrigued. I'm not intriguing. Just leave me alone."

"I can't help it. You're a flame and I'm the moth."

He stepped even closer, close enough that his chest was nearly touching her nose. She'd take one more step back and that was it. He might be at least twice her weight and width, but she could take him down if she had to. No

189

way was she going to let some beefed-up bully intimidate her. She took her step and made her stand with her sternest look.

"Did you just compare yourself to an insect?" She shook her head. "I'm not interested. I will never be interested. Please leave and don't ever seek me out again."

He reached toward her hair with a strange sappy look on his face like she'd just declared her love for him instead of slamming the proverbial door in his face. "You don't know me enough to know if you are interested."

She knocked his hand away. "I've heard enough about your pack to know I want nothing to do with them."

His whole body stiffened and the sappy mask fell from his face. "What have you heard?" he growled.

His soap or whatever it was and the diesel smell that followed him was bringing tears to her eyes. She waved her hand in front of her nose. "Back up and I'll tell you."

To her surprise, he immediately did what she asked.

She gripped the straps of her backpack in case she'd need to run. "Not only did your dad kick Zavier out of your pack, he forbade his parents to visit. I can understand your dad being afraid the curse might spread, but allowing Zavier's parents to visit wouldn't hurt anyone."

After some thought, she truly did understand the curse thing. Alpha Meyer was a weak alpha. Having someone in the pack with issues would have make it more difficult for him if what the guys said about rogues bringing down Zavier was true. He was probably feeling the curse in Zavier's head well before he kicked Zavier out.

"He was a drunk and a disgrace."

"So? He was still their child. If they were willing to love him despite that, your dad had no right to prevent it."

"He had every right. The alpha makes decisions for the good of the whole pack, not just one wolf. Zavier was a boil, a diseased limb. It was better to get rid of him with a clean cut then let the whole body wither away."

She was impressed by his analogy in spite of herself. "You have a surprising way with words, but it still doesn't make it right. Wouldn't you try to heal a diseased limb before lopping it off?"

"You don't think we tried?"

"Not when it counted. I was there, remember."

He stared at what she hoped was an invisible spot on her forehead. "You don't know the whole story."

"Tell me then."

He looked away from her and toward the clouds floating above the library as if they were the memories he was trying to pull up.

"We grew up together, obviously. He's only a year younger than me. He's also a cousin. Our parents planned that he would be my beta someday. I thought he would be, then somewhere in middle school, he decided he wanted to be more. He started throwing his power around and inciting other members of the pack against my brother and me. In high school it got even worse. I'd try to talk to him and he'd walk away like I didn't exist. Then in college, he sabotaged my relationship with the one girl I've ever wanted out of pure spite."

"Katie?" she asked.

His big head swung around and he squinted his eyes at her. "He told you about her?"

"Yeah. What happened to her?"

"She saw the light and drop-kicked his sorry ass to the curb."

191

"What did you tell her?"

If he was surprised she knew he'd done something, he didn't show it. "The truth; that he was only using her to get back at me."

Honey was pretty sure that wasn't all he told her. If she loved someone enough to marry them, she wouldn't believe anything a bully like Damien told her, unless it was something truly awful and he had proof.

"Is she a member of your pack?"

"No."

Which meant he had no power over her, except alpha power. Had he used it to force Katie to break up with Zavier or threatened her in some other way?

"You realize the break-up is the whole reason Zavier started drinking in the first place, right? If you hadn't interfered, he'd probably be happily married by now."

"That's his excuse. He's weak. If it hadn't been Katie it would have been something else. I saved her from him."

"He would have had only a few drinks if he hadn't been cursed."

"That's what he wants you to believe. Zavier's always had issues when it comes to alcohol and drugs."

He didn't smell like he was lying, but then, wolves could lie if they truly believed the lie. What if he was telling the truth? Would it put Walter in any danger? She made a note to scan him occasionally.

"Are you dating Katie now?"

"I'm not interested anymore. She…Zavier poisoned her against me."

That was a lie although she wasn't sure which part. Did Katie know what had happened to Zavier? Now that he was no longer part of Damien's pack maybe whatever had forced them apart no longer mattered.

"Have you talked to her lately?"

"No. Why would I?"

"Did you tell her what happened to Zavier? Did you tell her about the curse?"

"I'm sure she knows. It was all over social media."

"That he was cursed?"

Honey knew there were videos. She'd seen people filming at the scene. No one had been in wolf form so it wouldn't matter if humans saw the videos, but she doubted it was safe to bring up curses online.

Damien snorted. "Of course not. As far as the general public is concerned, the crazy attacker was locked away."

"I bet she feels really guilty. She probably thinks it's her fault Zavier went crazy."

He shrugged. "I doubt she cares. He got what he deserved for using her that way."

"Damien, are you that heartless? They were getting married. They loved each other. When two people love each other enough to promise the rest of their lives, they can't just turn it off even if one hurts the other."

"You're a romantic."

She slapped her palm against her forehead. She'd picked that up from Mom. Dad told her it was a nerdy thing to do, so she didn't do it around other people unless the situation really called for it. This one did. Besides, anything she could do to get Damien to leave her alone was a plus.

"I am human, well kind-of. I'm also a student. I have things to study. It's been interesting. Don't call me later." She took a quick look around. There were a few people

193

around but not many and they weren't paying attention to them.

"Honey, about our date on Friday…"

"What's that?" She looked down and stepped back like she'd seen a big spider. As soon as he looked down, she froze him. It was going to look a little weird for him to stand like that for thirty seconds, but it was much better than being frozen in the middle of a word. She ran away from the library and toward a place she was sure he wouldn't think to look for her – the clinic. She'd text the boys that Damien was hanging around again and if Walter came to get her, she'd take him out to dinner.

26

Honey

"What are you thinking about so hard?" Walter asked her. "You've barely said anything since you got in the car."

For once she was sitting in the front seat since only she and Walter had gone out to eat. It was nice not to have to put her feet on the hump in the back.

"Katie."

"Katie?"

"Yeah, Zavier's former fiancé. Someone should make sure she knows Zavier is all right so she doesn't live the rest of her life thinking she caused him to go crazy. I don't know how to contact her though."

"I could ask Zavier what her last name is," Walter said.

"No. I don't want to remind Zavier of her."

She debated contacting Zavier's mom, her aunt!, but she hadn't sounded very fond of Katie. That left Luna Lynn. She seemed to know everyone.

"I'll ask Lynn."

"Right now?" Walter asked when she pulled out her phone.

"What better time?"

The phone only rang twice before Lynn's worried voice sounded in her ear. "Honey, is something wrong?"

"No. Everything is fine. I just called to talk a little."

"Really?"

Honey wished she truly had so the doubt in Lynn's voice wouldn't be so justified. "And to ask what Katie's last name was."

"Katie?"

"Zavier's ex."

"Why do you want to know that?"

"I was talking with Damien and he said she probably didn't know that Zavier had been cursed. I thought someone should tell her so she won't feel guilty about what happened."

"Damien Meyer?" Lynn asked sharply.

"Yes."

"When did you talk to him?"

"An hour or so ago. He was on campus waiting for me after class."

"What did he want?"

"To take me on a date. I told him no."

"For the second time," Walter said loudly from the driver's seat.

"Who's that?" Lynn asked.

"Walter. We went out for dinner."

"With just Walter?"

"Yes. I thought it would be better if he wasn't on campus while Damien was."

"Why? Oh right, Walter is the one who joined Zavier's pack, isn't he. Smart. Other than this weekend, have you seen Damien any other time?"

"Yeah, Monday at training, he was a guest trainer."

"And that's it?"

"Monday at dinner," Walter said loudly, "but Honey wasn't there."

"Hmm. Let me know if he shows up again. He shouldn't be hanging around campus without a good reason."

"What about Katie? Do you know her last name and what pack she is from?" Honey asked.

"Honey, you are the sweetest child to worry about her. From what I understand, she broke it off with Zavier because she was more interested in following her career than settling down. I hear she got a scholarship to law school. It's my guess that she's counting her lucky stars that she broke it off when she did. Let her be. Zavier needs to focus on going forward, not looking back."

"I wasn't trying to get them back together. I just thought she should know."

"If she cares, she'll look into it herself."

Honey would have argued, but Lynn was already gushing about her plans for Christmas and it was impossible to get another word in.

"So, what are you going to get me?" Walter asked with a smirk after Honey had hung up the phone.

"Oh, you were expecting something?"

He scrunched his shoulders shyly. "Well, I thought, I mean, we are friends. I guess I could just take your gift back…"

She punched him. "You haven't gotten me anything."

"I have too."

"Really?"

"No, but I've thought about it."

She rolled her eyes. "You don't have to get me anything Walter. You've already done enough by helping Zavier."

"I want to. Besides, if I didn't, I'd look like the worst friend ever compared to the other guys."

"Well, don't get anything big. My mom and I usually just made each other gifts."

"You don't want me to make you something. Trust me."

They were nearly back on campus. She'd called Luca before they left the restaurant to make sure Damien wasn't hanging around. Luca said he wasn't but she decided to text him when they pulled into the parking lot to be sure. She needn't have bothered. Damien's gas-guzzler of a truck was parked in the student lot even though he was definitely not a student.

Walter parked in the first spot he saw, close to the street. "Now what?"

She was tired and she needed to finish studying for a test. Damien might be an alpha, but she lived in a dorm full of witches. He wouldn't be able to boss them around.

"I will find him and distract him. You need to get to your dorm."

"What if I don't want to go to my dorm?" Walter challenged.

"You have a quiz to study for and a class at 5:30 in the morning. Where else would you go?"

"What are you, my mother?"

"You're older than me. How would that happen?"

Walter's look turned serious. "I can't let you put yourself in danger for me."

"I won't be in any danger." She wiggled her fingers. "I have a gift, remember."

"You aren't invincible."

"I know."

"Call Brayton."

"This has nothing to do with him."

"Call Brayton. He's the future alpha of your pack. Protecting you from other future alphas is his responsibility."

"But we don't need him."

Walter reached over and touched her hand where it sat on the seat. "Honey, you have a secret that could cost you your life. I understand that sometimes you have to use your power, but if you can avoid it, you should. I know you're smart enough to know that. Call him. His mother has probably already ordered him to keep an eye on you anyway."

She hated that Walter was right. She picked up her phone and dialed Brayton, hoping he wouldn't answer. He was going to be grumpy or mad or scold her for something.

It took two rings.

"Honey? What's wrong?"

"Why would you think there's something wrong?"

"Your phone is on and you are calling me," he said in perfect deadpan.

"Have you seen Damien? His truck is in the parking lot. I'm with Walter."

"He's still hanging around? Stay there. I'll be right down. You're in Walter's car?"

"Yeah."

A few minutes later, Brayton, Rhys, Malcolm, and Cici spilled into the parking lot, looking around like they were soldiers on a mission. Rhys and Malcolm posted themselves where they could observe different points of entry (aka the sidewalks) while Cici and Brayton came right for Walter's car. Honey wanted to laugh. At the same time, she was relieved to see them.

Brayton opened her door. "Honey."

"Brayton." After a moment she added, "Thanks for coming."

He stood back while she pulled herself out of the car. "Why didn't you tell me you were being stalked?"

"I'm not being stalked. I just didn't want Damien anywhere near Walter."

He showed her his phone. "Mom says Damien showed up outside your class today."

"He did, but I got away."

Brayton gave her a stern look down his nose. She hadn't noticed it was so nicely shaped before. "Did you do what you did to him on Alpha Day? You know what I'm talking about. Don't deny it."

"Maybe."

"If you feel unsafe enough that you have to do that, there's a problem."

"He wasn't doing anything; I just didn't want him to follow me."

"Why are you defending him? Do you like him?" Cici snapped.

"No. I don't want things to get blown out of proportion is all."

"How did he know what classes you are in?" Cici asked.

Honey shrugged. "He could have asked someone in his pack. I'm friends with some of them. We've all talked about what we're taking."

"Do they know about Walter?" Brayton asked.

"No."

"They shouldn't," Walter cut in. "I've only been sitting with my pack members, well former pack members."

"S&P?" Honey asked.

Walter gave a nod. "S&P."

"It sounds like he's after Honey and not Walter, although he could be visiting someone in his pack," Brayton commented while he did another scan of the parking lot. "We need to figure out where he is and if he's a threat. We know he's not here, so Walter, you stay here with Rhys. I'll escort Honey to her dorm. Cici, you take Malcolm and go floor-by-floor in our dorm and make sure the path to Walter's room is clear."

"I should go with you to the girl's dorm," Cici said. "Boys aren't allowed to wander without an escort, but I can."

"Right. I forgot about that rule," Brayton said. "Tell your friends the plan, Walter, and to GT if you see him."

"GT?" Honey asked.

"Group Text."

Honey couldn't decide if she felt more like a soldier or a prisoner while she marched behind Brayton and in front of Cici down the sidewalk to her dorm. Damien wasn't waiting outside, nor was he in the lobby. He'd been there though. She could smell him.

"I can smell him too," Brayton said, noticing her sniffing. "There's something wrong with his truck."

"I bet he's upstairs," Cici said, heading for the elevator.

Honey went for the stairs. Brayton followed her. Cici sighed and followed them both with a roll of her eyes.

Half-way up the second flight of stairs, the smell got stronger. Brayton pushed past Honey, muttering "Stay here," under his breath. Cici was right on his heels. Honey felt silly standing in the middle of the stairwell. She chose to ignore Brayton's order and follow them up to the top of the stairs where she could peer around the corner into the hallway. Brayton and Cici and a girl way at the end of the hall were the only people in sight. Brayton stomped up to Honey's door and pounded on it with his fist. She couldn't see who opened it, but Brayton stopped pounding and looked down.

"Are you okay?" he asked.

Honey didn't hear the response, but Brayton puffed up and said very loudly, loud enough that every girl on the floor could hear, "Damien, get out here."

A few moments later Damien sauntered out of the room. He was puffy too. His cologne smell in the cramped hallway made her feel sick to her stomach.

"Why are you in Honey's room?" Brayton demanded. She wondered how he knew it was her room. For that matter, how did Damien know where her room was?

"I was chatting with her roommate. That's not a crime."

"No, but stalking is."

"I'm not stalking her."

"Did Honey tell you where her room was or what classes she was taking?"

"It wasn't classified information. Besides, we're fated. It's inevitable that we will be together."

"What are you talking about?"

"She smelled me. She said she could smell my cologne. I'm not wearing cologne. You know what that means. She's my mate."

What an idiot. Honey clamped her hand over her nose and stomped down the hallway. "I am not!"

Damien looked her way and chuckled. "Then why are you holding your nose?"

"Because you stink. It's making me feel sick."

"What does he smell like?" Brayton asked.

"Like really cheap, nasty cologne. Cloying. That's how I'd describe it." She waved her hand in front of the other hand that was still holding her nose. "It's worse when you're trying to out-alpha someone. Can you turn it off?"

"Maybe you're smelling his alpha power," Brayton said.

"Yours doesn't smell. You just poof up."

"Pardon?" Damien said.

"All the alphas do. Whenever you use your power, you poof up like male turkeys or peacocks when they try to make themselves look big."

Cici snorted even though her head was bowed from the pressure the two alphas were putting on her.

"What is she talking about?" Damien demanded.

"Being a rogue her whole life has affected her brain," Brayton said. "She doesn't react to things the way other wolves do. Instead of feeling alpha power, she apparently sees it, and now smells it."

"You're lying."

"You can smell I'm not. It's damn annoying too. The girl doesn't know how to listen."

"I do too," Honey protested.

Brayton shot her a smug look. "Then why aren't you waiting on the stairs like I told you?"

Like she would stand there and let Damien claim her as his mate. "Because there were things that needed to be said."

Brayton waved his hand in her direction. "See what I mean. Damien, I would love for her to be your fated, then you could take her off our hands, but I don't think it's the case. You haven't said that she smells good to you and neither one of you is acting besotted. I think it's just another one of Honey's oddities."

"I'm not odd."

Her across-the-hall witch neighbor poked her head out her door. "Um yeah, you are."

Ouch. Maybe she wasn't the friend Honey thought she was.

Her neighbor poked her head out again, "I mean that in the best way, Honey. You are a good kind of odd. My favorite odd wolf, in fact." She shot her a grin and ducked back into her room.

"Thanks."

"Why are there so many damn witches around here?" Damien grumbled.

"Because this is where they stay. I'm the only wolf in the dorm," Honey replied.

Damien shook his head. "I need to be going. I have stuff to do. I'll see you around Brayton."

"Sure."

The elevator door had just shut on Damien when Honey remembered. "Oh no, we have to warn…."

Cici shook her phone at her. "I sent a text as soon as I saw him. They'll be fine."

27

Honey

Saturday morning, Honey jogged over to the clinic to follow Dr. Ziga for a few hours. She still wasn't sure if she wanted to go into medicine, but she did enjoy learning about it. On her way back, she texted the boys that she was going to the library again. She wasn't really surprised to find one of them waiting for her at the entrance, but she *was* surprised it was Liam. He'd watched the Friday night movie too. Maybe he'd decided he liked her again?

She gave him one of her biggest smiles. "Good morning."

A smile broke through his serious facade. "Good morning to you, Honey, although it's getting close to afternoon."

"Not yet though."

"You don't have your backpack. Why are you here? I figured you were studying."

"Come on, I'll show you."

She led him up to the top floor and back to the shelves where the yearbooks were. He followed her without a word. He probably thought she was going to get a book on magic.

The two books she wanted were still there. She pulled them out and headed for the open study space.

"Where do you want to sit, on a cushy chair or at a desk or…in a window seat?" She flicked her eyes between him and the window seat suggestively. It was easily big enough for two.

"Cushy couch is fine. Why are you looking at yearbooks?"

"I'm trying to find my mom."

"Is that why you were in the library Monday?"

"Yeah. Isn't this place great? I didn't know this study area was here until then."

He looked around. "It's not bad. It'd be even better if it wasn't so cloudy outside."

The clouds were so low and heavy it looked like the buildings were holding them up. "Think it will snow finally?"

"The weatherman said so."

"Yeah, but he's been wrong the last three times."

"You like snow then?"

"Yes." She plopped down on a reddish-orange couch and pulled open the book for the year when her mom would have been a sophomore. "Don't you?"

He sat down on the matching armchair and dropped his backpack on the floor beside him. "Eh." Instead of pulling out a book, he reached for the other yearbook. "You sure she'll be in this one? I thought she had you right after college."

"She was a freshman that year. I already looked for her in the other two years."

He started flipping through his book, so she started going through hers.

Honey found her first. Her mom's wavy hair was longer than she'd ever seen her wear it, and her face was a little rounder, but otherwise, she looked exactly as Honey remembered – exactly like she had the day Honey had attended her single day of high school.

She thought she'd prepared herself. It was just a picture. She knew there was a chance she'd see her mom, but she was sobbing before she realized the tears were coming. Her mom's smiling, happy face morphed into a motionless body on the floor. Her clothes were burning, but her face was untouched. If there'd been any hope she was alive, she would have tried to save her, but there was no life in her eyes.

"Honey, Honey, it's all right. Shhh. I've got you."

She didn't know how long Liam sat there with his arms around her and his head on top of hers. She didn't even remember him moving to sit beside her, but she was glad he was there.

Eventually, she got her tears under control. Her face was a mess, as was his jacket. She tried to wipe it off with her arm, but she only managed to smear the moisture around.

"Sorry."

He pushed the strands of hair that had escaped from her ponytail off her wet cheeks and tucked them behind her ear, then wiped her cheeks with his thumb. "It's okay. If anyone has the right to cry, it's you. Which one is she?"

He nodded to the book on the low table in front of the couch. She didn't remember putting it there, but it was a good thing she had, else it would be dripping wet. She wiped her hand on her shirt and pointed. "That's her."

"Her name was Madeline?"

"Apparently. I didn't know."

"Madeline Wixx."

"It doesn't sound like her at all. It's too stern and proper." Her nose was threatening to drip. "I'm going to go wipe my face."

"I'll be here."

The good thing about the modern decor in this part of the library, although truthfully, this floor wasn't as bad as the others, were the very obvious signs that hung down from the ceilings next to the bathrooms. She took her time blowing her nose and splashing cold water over her face. It was only when she went to dry off that she realized there were no paper towels in the holder or anywhere. Dripping, she poked her head outside to see if there was a janitor's closet. There was, at least she assumed that's what the nondescript door was next to the men's restroom. It wasn't locked. She opened the door and peered inside. It was just large enough to step inside and there were stacks of paper towels high on a shelf and toward the back.

The smell of magic greeted her as soon as she crossed the threshold. She thought at first that a witch had used the closet to perform magic where no one would see, but the hairs on her right arm tingled when she reached up for the towels. The back wall was a door? Since she could sense it, did that mean she could still get in? She looked over her shoulder to make sure no one was standing outside the closet, then poked the wall. A spark shot from her finger and split into multiple branches that shot in all directions across the surface of the wall. Several inches from the corner, the branches turned sharply and ran in straight lines in both directions until they'd traced the outline of a small door. With a final blue shimmer, a shining blue doorknob appeared, just like the one she'd seen before.

It still worked! She could still get in! She didn't reach for the knob though. Liam was waiting for her and if she opened that door, he'd smell it. Later. She'd come back later after she'd had something to eat and she had plenty of time to browse. She'd have to make sure there was time to shower afterward too, or maybe she could use her own power to block the magical stench from sticking to her. Would the witches be able to tell she was using her power with all the other magical residue in the library?

"Honey, what are you doing?" Liam said from outside the door.

The door to the magical library vanished right when his shadow blocked off the weak light from the hall.

"Looking for paper towels." she waved the package she had in her hand. "I'll go put these in the bathroom."

"What are you, the janitor now?" he teased when she slipped by him.

"No, I just thought I'd make it easier for the next person who has a sobbing fit to dry their face without using their shirt."

"Good idea. You might want to keep a few of those."
"Why?"

He pointed toward the big windows. "It's snowing and you're going to get all wet walking back across campus. Why aren't you wearing a coat?"

"I thought if I didn't, it would snow. See, it worked."

He rolled his eyes, but his mouth had an upturn to it. Was Liam finally starting to thaw?

28

Honey

Sunday was warmer than it had been all week. The dusting of snow they'd received the day before quickly disappeared. She and Walter walked to church, then went to brunch with a few human college students they'd met at church. Walter hadn't spent much time around humans. The Little pack was so large they had their own high school, but he got along with the people at church just fine. In fact, she was certain a couple of the girls would have gone out with him if he'd asked.

"You going to come by to study later?" Walter asked as they walked back.

"Yeah. I thought I'd swing by the library for a little while first."

"The library? I thought you found your mom."

"I did. I'm looking for something else."

"Something magical, perhaps?" he said knowingly.

"Maybe."

He put his arm around her shoulder and squeezed. "I don't have a problem with that. You can't help what you are any more than I can help these," he tapped his glasses. "Just be careful, okay. Don't give yourself away. You're one of my best friends and I don't want anything to happen to you."

She'd never had anyone call her a best friend before. She put her arm around his waist and leaned her head against him in a kind of half-hug. "Thank you, Walter."

He squeezed her again, then let go.

"Can I ask you a question," she said.

"Sure."

"Why doesn't Liam like me anymore?"

Walter sighed. He was silent so long she thought he wasn't going to answer, but then he did.

"It's not that he doesn't like you. You have to understand, Honey, everyone knows that the offspring of a witch and a wolf is a monster and a curse. It's so taboo to even interact with a witch that even a decade ago just talking to a witch could get you thrown out of some packs. Did you know this is one of only a few colleges in the country where wolves and witches go to school together? Witches were allowed in as part of the treaty but it wasn't well-received. What you are goes against everything we've ever been taught. Liam's worried for you, and for us. You are supposed to be cursed and anyone who knows what you are and doesn't report it is supposedly cursed too."

"Cursed how?"

"Birth defects, really bad ones. If the babies live they're violent and uncontrollable. That's why they're supposed to be put down. If the parents and the people who know about the child don't put it down then they are liable and can be sued."

"The curse is a legal action?"

213

"That's what it is now, so people don't feel the wrath of the actual curse which is apparently much worse."

She crossed her arms. How could people be so stupid? "I'm not cursed, nor am I a monster."

"Liam is afraid you might be using magic on us to, well, lead us into a situation where the curse will make itself known in a devastating fashion."

"I'm not. I wouldn't."

"Not on purpose – as part of your curse."

"You'd be able to smell it."

"I know Honey. I don't think he's right. After what you did for Brayton and Zavier, I suspect you're unaffected because of your specific kind of magic."

"What do you mean?"

"Witches have different powers, right? I think yours is some kind of protective magic. I think it must have or is still shielding you from the curse and has been your whole life."

"Did you tell Liam?"

"I did."

"And?"

"He's researching."

"Meanwhile, he doesn't want to hang around me because he thinks I'm cursed and he's afraid it will rub off on him?"

"Something like that."

She was angry, but at the same time, it felt like her heart was ripping in two. "Do you think he'll report me?"

"No. He knows what would happen if he did and none of us want that. Plus, so far there's no evidence that you're cursed or that you've cursed us."

"My parents died."

214

"True, but other than that did they have an unnatural amount of bad luck?"

"No."

"Not all bad things that happen are due to a curse."

"Would you turn me in?"

He stopped and turned her by her shoulders so she was looking at him. "No. The only way I'd ever turn you in Honey, if is you actually turned into a monster and started killing people, or attempted to, and then I'd capture you and try to fix you first."

She threw both arms around him this time. "If I did start trying to harm people, please do whatever you need to do to stop me. I don't want to hurt anyone."

He hugged her back. "I know."

Walter walked her all the way to the library, then gave her another hug before leaving her at the front door. She ran up the stairs to the top floor and popped out breathless and hopeful. There were only four other people on the top floor of the library, all of them well away from the corner where she'd first found the door. She decided to try there before going to the janitor's closet since it was more hidden. The closet would be plan B.

She casually wandered back to the corner with the ancient couch. With one last look to make sure no one was paying attention, she touched the wall. Nothing happened. She tried touching it in another spot. Still nothing. She didn't smell magic anymore either. Had the librarian simply moved the door, or had she figured out how to keep her out?

She followed the wall toward the janitor's closet while keeping her senses opened for smells or tingles in case the door had simply shifted a few feet. All she smelled were books and dust and whatever they used to clean the bathrooms until she reached the janitor's closet. It was very faint, but there was definitely magic. Unfortunately the closet was locked. How funny, yet not funny. She could get through magic but not a human invention.

Honey tried the knob again. How did the witches get in? Did they all know a spell to unlock doors? Did they all have a key? That would be ridiculous. There were at least a thousand witches on campus and they wouldn't even know the door had changed unless they visited the library and realized they were locked out.

The magical library was big. There was bound to be another door somewhere. She could search for that or spy on the door until someone went in or figure out how to pick a lock or she could find the janitor and have him or her unlock the door and freeze them, then slip by and …

No. It was strictly forbidden to use magic on humans unless it was for their safety. Her mom had taught her that from the time she was old enough to understand. Anyone who used magic on humans or wolves to further their own purposes was a monster, plain and simple. It was one of the major reasons humans despised witches back when they knew they existed. It was the reason wolves hated them too.

So much for her hour of magical exploration.

She took a step away, then turned back. Maybe there was code word. "Alohomora? Open Sesame? Aliese? Please?"

Nothing.

"Dang it." She twisted the knob as hard as she could. "Open!"

The knob fell off in her hand. Oops. Any guilt she felt was quickly replaced by elation. She looked around to make sure no one was paying attention to her, then slipped inside the dark closet. It smelled just like it had before – magical. She put the doorknob on the shelf and turned to the back wall. Blue lightning shot out when she touched the surface. It didn't hurt as much this time, or perhaps she was just getting used to it. She was half-afraid the door that materialized in front of her would be locked too, but when she turned the knob it opened easily. She turned her head and took a deep breath of mostly magic-free air and stepped inside.

Somehow, even though the door had moved to another wall on the non-magical side, she ended up in the same spot she'd been before. Cool. She didn't know witches had powers like that. Maybe she could find a book listing all the different types of powers. At least it would give her something to ask the librarian for if she showed up again.

She started her exploration by perusing the titles nearest the door. It appeared to be the travel section. You could take guided tours of cursed tombs around the world or places of power in Europe. There was also a whole row of books in eye-watering orange and green that started with 'My trip to…', all by the same author. Further along, the titles morphed into a description of culture. Some of the books were so old-looking she was surprised they weren't considered history books. At the back of the broader balcony on the end, she found a display shelf with catalogs from different magical colleges, including her own. The catalog looked different from all the other ones she'd seen. She picked it up, expecting it to be for a different year, but it wasn't. Instead of the normal departments, it was specifically for the college of witchcraft and healing.

They had a whole college of witchcraft? She knew they had classes specifically for witches, but she didn't realize there was a whole college, nor did she realize the witches could earn witch-related degrees. When she had asked her witch friends about their degrees, they always said something very normal sounding like business or journalism. She guessed they felt it would be odd to say they were getting a degree in alchemical science or mystical healing.

"How did you get in here?"

The librarian's voice made Honey jump. The woman didn't sound happy.

"Through the door."

"Which one?"

Ha, she knew there were more. Honey didn't say that though.

"The one between the bathrooms."

"How did you find it?"

"I was looking for paper towels for the bathroom and I smelled the magic."

"Wasn't the closet door locked?"

"It opened."

The librarian muttered something foreign-sounding under her breath, then said, "You really shouldn't be in here. There's nothing on these shelves that is of interest to a wolf."

"Not true." Honey pointed to the page she was reading in the catalog. "What classes would I need to get

218

an associate's degree in magical history and where would I take the classes?"

The librarian raised an eyebrow at her. "You want to get a degree in magical history?"

"Maybe. What's involved?"

The librarian let out a long-suffering sigh. "It's a self-study course. Your read the books, take an exam, and then write a thesis paper on a topic of your choice. If you pass, you get the degree."

"How many books?" Honey asked.

"There are three total."

"Is there a time limit?"

"You can take a hundred years if you want."

"How do I enroll?"

"If you were a witch, I would enroll you. It would show up as an elective on your transcript, but since you aren't a witch, you can't enroll in the class."

"Why not?"

"Because you aren't a witch," the librarian said as if that was all the argument she needed.

"That reason is illegal due to its discriminatory nature," Honey argued back, "and I may not be what you normally classify as a witch, but I do have magic. All wolves do."

The librarian's lips compressed into a thin line, but Honey wasn't about to back down.

"In order to enroll in the college, you also need to be a member of a coven AND you had to have helped with the craft fair," the librarian spouted smugly.

"Good thing I helped my witch friends set up their booths then. I'll ask my roommate if I can join her coven. If she says yes, can I enroll?"

219

"Your roommate?" the librarian frowned at her.

"Yeah."

"Your roommate is a witch?"

"Yes."

"Well, just because she says you can be in her coven doesn't mean you can. All of the witches have to agree."

"Most of her friends are my friends so I don't think it will be a problem."

The librarian threw up her hands. "Fine, if you can find a coven who will accept you and bring some proof that you helped with the fair, I'll let you enroll." She shook her finger at Honey's nose. "It won't be easy though. This is not one of those gym classes you wolves are so fond of."

"I like challenges. Would it be possible for me to check out a book today?"

"No. You cannot check out any books unless you are enrolled in the college."

"Do you have an introductory book on alchemical science I can look at while I'm here?"

"What do you want with that?"

"I want to read it."

The librarian closed her eyes for a moment, then spun on her heel and stomped toward the spiral staircase. Honey assumed she was supposed to follow. They went four floors down and stopped one floor above the ground floor. The librarian pulled out a thin, hard-back book with a ratty green cover and thrust it at her. "Here. This should cover the basics."

"Thank you."

"Just leave it out when you're done. I'll reshelve it."

"Yes, ma'am."

It was basically a picture book. It didn't take her long to finish. Alchemical scientists used magic to transform molecules from one substance to another, in theory. The book made it sound like a wonderful skill to have, even though nothing could be transformed permanently.

Human chemistry made a lot more sense.

She still had half-an-hour of the time she'd allotted herself, so she started scanning the bookshelves again. She'd barely gone ten feet when she found a blue textbook with white lettering that made the smells and sounds and sights of the rest of the world fade. Had she finally found someone else with a power like hers? Reverently, she pulled "The Magic of Molecules" off the shelf and returned to the chair where she'd been sitting before.

The book reminded her of her chemistry book. In fact, a lot of the concepts and terminology were the same, but where human chemistry had always seemed a bit cloudy to her, this book explained it with magic – very detailed, very exact magic which she had no trouble applying to the picture of how molecules worked and looked already in her head. She dove in.

Her mom had taught her a lot of general things about magic, but she hadn't been able to teach her anything specific since her talent was completely different. For the first time, Honey felt like she was learning something about her own skill.

An hour later, she reluctantly shut the book. She had actual classes to study for and a shower to take so the guys wouldn't complain about her smell. She debated leaving the blue book on the table, but she wanted to make sure she knew where it was the next time she visited, so she put it back.

The librarian was nowhere to be seen, nor was anyone else. Keeping an eye and an ear out, she started a casual walk around the balcony. There had to be another door somewhere.

There were, in fact, a lot of doors. One on each balcony. She could see them all if she stood exactly opposite the door on her balcony. Where did they all go? There were more floors in this library than the modern one since the balconies were stacked so tightly, which meant some of the doors would pop out in the middle of a floor or even between. Curious, she walked around the balcony and opened the one on her floor. She opened it but did not step through. The smell of smoke coming from the dark doorway wasn't strong, but it was exactly the same smell she smelled when she found her parents; the same smell she'd worn on her clothes for days and smelled in her nightmares for weeks afterward. She slammed it shut and headed for the stairs.

29

Honey

Between studying, going to the gym to work on her arm strength, and sneaking into the library to read the Magic of Molecules, the weeks sped by. Suddenly it was December thirteenth, her birthday, her first birthday without Mom.

She was not going to cry, not today. Her mom wouldn't want her to cry. She'd tell her to look at the bright things; to see what was in the glass instead of what was missing. That was really hard to do when what was missing was a pile of her mom's homemade birthday pancakes with strawberries and whip cream. She made herself get out of bed and get ready. Mom wouldn't have made breakfast pancakes at five in the morning anyway.

She'd told the guys once when her birthday was, but they must have forgotten, because not at single one of them wished her happy birthday, not even when they were walking back to the dorm from WOLF. Nobody in her pack said anything either, not even Charlize.

Honey took her shower and dropped by the cafeteria. No pancakes. They did have big chocolate muffins with chocolate chunks and some fresh strawberries. She made it work.

Every single one of her teachers spent the entire class reviewing for final exams. Honey was nervous, but she knew she could do it. Her mom had given her final exams all the time to toughen her up, she'd said. Mom's exams were hard and if she did bad, Honey had to do the dishes for a month by herself. Honey never failed, so she didn't know if Mom would have actually made her do them.

After her last class she went to the witch's library again. It was her birthday after all. Once she was in the janitor's closet, she locked a thin layer of air molecules around her to keep the magical smells from clinging to her. It didn't take much effort. She just had to remember not to relax her control. From practicing around her dad, she knew the air shield also blocked the faint smell of the magic that she used to create it from other wolves. She didn't know if it worked on witches since they detected wolves and other witches by feel instead of smell, but she figured there was so much magic floating around in the library, her weak signature would get lost. If she had to, she could always claim she was wearing a spell, which was true.

The Magic of Molecules was right where she'd left it. She turned to the fifth chapter and pulled out her notebook. She might not be able to check the book out, but there were no rules against taking notes, she hoped.

When the sentences started to run together, which was sadly less than an hour, she put the book back and gathered her things. Every time she visited, she explored a different part of the library. This time, she decided to go down to the very bottom floor.

Unlike the other floors, the walls of the bottom floor weren't covered floor to ceiling in books. Only the bottom half of the walls had shelves and they held sets of books instead of the mishmash of volumes the other floors had. Candles, crystals, small cauldrons and the burners to heat them were scattered between the books. A few items, like a big glass ball that emanated power, had places of distinction on top of the shelves. From the electrical smell, she guessed the ball's purpose was to store and provide power. Getting near to it felt like standing close to the hidden door right before it shocked her, only a lot worse. She kept several feet between her and the ball.

Above the shelves, the walls were covered with photographs and oil paintings. Many of the photographs were yellowed with age and faded around the edges. She started reading the labels, expecting them to be from the late 1800s based on the clothes, but there was one as early as 1850. The photo showed four women sitting in chairs in front of five standing men who were posing with cups and saucers like they were having a tea party. It was labeled "Founding members of Wiccan Academy, 1850" and listed the names. That the academy was older than the college and that both women and men were responsible for founding it was interesting enough, but the young couple, or possibly brother and sister, on the left-most side of the picture had her mother's last name. Their names were Anthony and Victoria Wixx.

She couldn't see any resemblance between herself and her mother or them, but the picture had been taken several generations ago. She moved on to the rest of the pictures. Every-so-often, the Wixx name popped up again, sometimes associated with men, but more often with women. There was a picture of a ground-breaking in 1860 and she wondered if that was the building she was standing in now. She eventually came to some more recent photos displayed on top of a shelf.

Her heart jumped into her throat. One of them was her mom. She was wearing a mortarboard hat and a huge smile and holding a single rose and a rolled-up piece of paper. She looked young and happy. Next to that was a large picture, this one of an entire class. Honey guessed it was the graduating witches since the group looked too small to be the entire graduating class of the college. She recognized the woman standing next to her mom too.

"Back again?"

The sharp voice of that same woman made her jump at least half a foot. It was a good thing she wasn't holding the picture else she might have dropped it. Honey was beginning to think the librarian got a kick out of seeing how far she could make her jump. Honey put on a smile so the woman wouldn't know how much her stealth irritated her and so she could try to wheedle some information from her.

"I am. It's really nice you have all these pictures. I didn't realize the witch's college went back so far. It's neat that the same family names keep showing up over and over." Honey walked back over to the oldest photograph. "I noticed the Wixx name popped up a lot. Were the founders brother and sister or were they married?"

"Brother and sister." The librarian narrowed her eyes at Honey. "Why do you care?"

"I like history."

226

"What do you know about the Wixxes?"

"Nothing. I just noticed the name because it's unique. It's not very often you see two x's in a row."

The librarian's suspicious demeanor relaxed slightly. "You were looking at one of their descendants." She nodded toward Honey's mom's picture.

"She's pretty."

Hopefully the librarian didn't notice how closely Honey resembled her.

The librarian's gaze flicked between Honey and the picture of her mom. "You look a lot like her."

"We both have brown hair," Honey concurred.

The librarian let out a huff that could have been a snort. "Don't worry, I know you aren't related. She's from one of the most prominent families in the witching world and you are a wolf."

"Prominent?"

"Have you truly never heard of the Wixx family?" She walked past Honey and picked up her mother's picture. "They can trace their ancestry to one of the first known witch families. The name is so famous, men take the Wixx name when they marry into the family instead of the other way around."

"No, I haven't heard of them. Why are they famous? What does the family do for a living?"

The names of powerful families tended to turn up in history books despite the need to keep their powers secret. They couldn't seem to stay away from politics and business.

"I guess you wouldn't have heard of them. In the witching world, everyone knows who they are. Their powers are legendary. Most of the wards and special

227

magics of the library were designed by them. Victoria and her brother made some we still use today. Madeline here," the librarian nodded at Honey's mom's picture, "was one of the strongest healers born in this century."

"Really?"

"Oh yes. She could actually heal a broken bone. Most healers can only get the healing process started."

"Was? What happened to her?"

Did the librarian know her mom was gone? How could she? Was she involved somehow?

The librarian put the picture back down on the shelf. "No one knows. She disappeared. She said she was going to travel the world before she settled down. She sent a few postcards, but they eventually stopped coming."

She said it matter-of-factly, but she sounded sad.

"Were you her friend?" Honey pointed to the other picture. "I noticed you were next to her in this picture."

"I thought I was, but after graduation," the librarian sighed. "Why am I telling you this? Did you find a coven yet?"

Honey had showed the woman the notes from her friends saying she helped at the fair but the librarian insisted she had to find a coven too. Honey suspected they both knew that wasn't going to happen. Blaze was very nice about it, but she said no because she knew she'd get kicked out of her current coven if she sponsored a wolf and starting their own coven required a sponsor. "No, but I haven't been looking. Finals are next week."

"And yet you are here."

"Studying," Honey pointed out. "I found a magical chemistry book. The explanations in there make more sense to me than the human ones, although I can't, of course, use those on my exam."

"I should say not."

"Still, it's interesting. I'm double majoring in chemistry and physics because this college doesn't have a chemical physics degree, but now that I've seen that book, I'm wondering how much magic plays a role in the physics of chemical reactions and if it's possible to explain it in a way that humans wouldn't recognize it for what it is."

The woman blinked at Honey. "You're a chemistry major?"

"And physics."

"Then why were you bothering me about a magical history degree?"

"I like history too. You said it was self-paced. I figured I could read the books over winter break and work on the paper a couple of hours every week."

The librarian frowned at Honey like she didn't believe her. "What was your high school GPA?"

"I didn't go to high school. I was home-schooled."

"Wolves are home-schooled?"

Honey shrugged. "I was."

"How old are you?"

"Not yet 18."

It wasn't the question. It was remembering that it was her birthday and that her friends had forgotten that brought tears to her eyes. That and she'd just been talking about Mom to a friend she'd never known Mom had; one whom her mother had likely abandoned because of her. She turned away from the librarian before the tears could escape her eyes.

"I better go. My friends will be wondering where I am."

Mentioning her friends was not a good way to get control of her tears.

The lights in the library all pulsed brightly for a moment and a faint gong sounded, although Honey couldn't say exactly where the sound originated from. "What was that?"

The librarian looked up toward the door Honey usually came in and blew the strand of hair that had come lose from her bun off her face. "A wolf trying to get in."

"Does the library do that when I come in?"

The librarian looked at Honey through the corner of her eye. "No, which makes me wonder what kind of protective talisman you're wearing. That's what it *should* do."

"Oh."

They stood there for several seconds, Honey waiting to see what the librarian would do and the librarian waiting to see if the doorbell rang again.

"Shall I go see who it is?" Honey finally asked.

"Did you tell anyone about the door or where to find you?" the librarian asked sharply.

"No, of course not. All I ever say is that I'm going to study in the library."

"We'll just wait then. He or she won't remember what they were doing by the closet and wander away. I put a forgetful ward on the closet door so any non-witches who touch it won't remember why they were there."

"Isn't that illegal, to perform magic on a wolf?"

The librarian lifted her finger, not to point, just to emphasize her words. "I performed magic on the door, not a wolf, and the magic is not targeted at wolves, just non-witches."

"What about the janitor?"

"The janitor is a witch."

"Oh," Honey said again.

They waited. Honey had turned to look at photos again by the time the librarian finally spoke.

"It's probably safe to leave. Make sure the hallway is empty before you step out."

"Yes, Ma'am."

The library gonged again. Footsteps clattered on the spiral steps behind them. A few moments later, two girls, one short and slightly plump and one tall and skinny, spilled off the stairs and came rushing toward them. The short one had blond, curly hair and pink cheeks. The tall one had straight, dark hair and tanned skin that spoke of an Indian heritage: India Indian, not Native American Indian.

"What's happening?" the blonde asked breathlessly. "Are we under attack?"

"No. It's just the perimeter alarm," the librarian said in a much kinder manner than Honey had ever heard her use. "It's been going off more since I moved the door. A lot of people brush past it on accident."

"Is there another door? I can go look and see what's going on," Honey volunteered.

The librarian gave Honey a look that said she knew Honey was only volunteering so she could find another door. The blonde girl looked at Honey like she was crazy.

"It's too dangerous! There are wolves out there."

Apparently, her air-shield did work on witches, at least in the library.

231

"They'll get kicked out of school if they attack me on school property. Besides," Honey dropped into a fighting stance, "I know karate."

"But wolves are big and strong and you're, well, you're," the blond girl looked her up and down, "fit."

"I go to the gym."

Honey could have sworn the librarian snorted, but she had her sour-face on when Honey looked back at her. "Fine. Go up two floors and use the red door on this side. It's a one-way emergency door, so don't try to come back in that way. You'll exit on the second floor in the closet where the printing supplies are stored. The door won't open unless the room is empty."

That seemed like an odd feature for an emergency door, but Honey didn't say that.

"There's no need to report back. I'll know if you are successful."

"Yes Ma'am."

Honey popped out of the wall right where the librarian said she would. The red door was gone when she looked back. The ozone from the nearby printers made it hard to smell the magic from the library, but she could still smell it a little. Oh right. She released her air shield along with the magical residue from the library that coated it. The ozone smell was strong enough she knew any wolves in the area wouldn't be able to detect a thing, which was probably why the door was hidden where it was.

She found a set of stairs and ran all the way up to the top floor. The bell ringer had to be Liam. He was the only one she'd introduced to the top floor and he'd been suspicious of the closet. Also, she'd texted the boys to tell them she was going to the library for a while. Maybe he'd remembered it was her birthday.

It wasn't Liam. It wasn't even one of the guys.

She slipped silently across the floor to where Brayton was eyeing the closet from the entrance of the short hallway. "What are you doing?"

He sprang at least two feet into the air. No wonder the librarian enjoyed making her jump so much.

He spun around angrily as soon as he landed. "Honey! Don't do that!"

She figured he'd shake her or something when he grabbed her shoulders, but he pulled her into a tight hug and laid his head against hers with a sigh. "Happy birthday."

She would have hugged him back just for remembering, but her arms were pinned to her sides. She couldn't believe it was Brayton who remembered and not her friends.

"You remembered?"

He released her from the hug and stepped back but kept his hands on her shoulders. "How could I forget when Mom has been bugging me about the plans for the last three weeks? I think she's made more effort for your birthday than she ever did for one of mine. And You. Are. Ruining. It. Because you have your phone off again." He shook her with each word.

"No I don't." She shrugged his hands off her shoulders and pulled her phone out of her backpack to show him.

He took it and scowled at the screen. She was glad she wasn't the phone.

233

"Whatever." He tossed it back to her. "Come on, everyone is waiting."

She jogged to catch up with him. "Waiting where?"

"The cafeteria. Mom thought it would be nice to combine your birthday with an end-of-the semester celebration. She had the cafeteria people bake a huge chocolate cake for dessert and lasagna and salad because you seem to like salad."

"Is she there?" Honey asked.

"Yes."

"Oh. I'm sorry for keeping everyone waiting. I texted the boys where I was."

"I know."

He was walking so fast she had to run to stay beside him. "Why did you come to look for me and not my friends?"

He stopped abruptly and shot her a hard look. "Am I not a friend?"

"I…I guess. You just don't seem to like me very much."

He started walking again. "I like you fine Honey."

She chased after him almost to the parking lot by the cafeteria before she asked the question that was really on her mind. "Why were you trying to get into the janitor's closet when I found you?" Had Liam told him where to look?

He stopped again and gave her a piercing look that threatened to pin her tongue down. "Why do you think I was trying to get into the janitor's closet?"

"Because you were looking at it."

"I could have been looking at the girl's bathroom and trying to decide if I should knock on the door or not since

I'd already searched the rest of the library." He nearly yelled the last few words.

"But you weren't," she persisted.

He took a step toward her. He didn't look like he was starting to inflate, but she suspected he wanted to.

"Where were you Honey?"

"Looking at pictures on the ground floor."

"You weren't on the ground floor."

"I was." It was the absolute truth. She knew he knew it since she could hear him sniffing the air.

"Why did you go to the top floor then?"

"Nope. You have to answer my question first. Why were you looking at the closet Brayton?" She wasn't quite sure why she persisted, other than it was fun to ruffle his fur.

His stern look morphed into a cocky little half-smile that made her stomach feel strange and he stepped even closer. "I think we both know why I was looking at the closet."

He was too close. His body spray was making it hard to breath. She took a step back. "Um, no we don't."

"You feel it too, don't you?"

"Feel what?"

He tilted his head like he was trying to puzzle something out. "You're eighteen today, right?"

"No."

"Seventeen?"

"No."

"You're sixteen?" he asked incredulously.

"No."

All color washed from his face. "Don't tell me you're fourteen."

"I was."

He closed his eyes. "Does mom know?"

"Yeah."

"And your friends?"

"Liam does. He kind of guessed. I haven't told the others yet. I was afraid they'd treat me different if they knew. I think maybe it's time though."

Brayton abruptly pulled her into another hug, pinning her arms to her sides again. When he didn't move for several seconds, it started to feel weird.

"Brayton, what are you doing?"

He finally let go of her only to put his hands on her shoulders again. At least he didn't shake her. "Why didn't you tell me?"

"What difference did it make?"

"I wouldn't have...I would have treated you better."

"No. You would have treated me like a kid. You would have ignored me and bossed me around and told everyone else to treat me like a kid. I wouldn't have had any friends at all."

"I wouldn't have done that."

"Yes, Brayton. You would have," she knew that without a doubt.

He sighed, then abruptly planted a gentle kiss to the side of her head. "You're amazing Honey. I hurt you and acted like a jerk and you helped me anyway. You've handled everything that's been thrown at you with more maturity than most people *my* age would do. I am proud to have you in my pack and would be even prouder to call you my friend." He slid his hands down her arms to take her hands. "Will you be my friend? No, will you let me be *your* friend?"

It was an oddly formal way to start a friendship. She wasn't sure exactly what he was asking for. "Does that mean you want to come to movie night?"

He threw back his head and laughed. "Maybe. Would I get to pick the movie?"

"When it's your turn."

He laughed again even while he turned and started dragging her across the parking lot.

30

Honey

It was the biggest birthday party she'd ever had. Considering all her other parties consisted only of Mom and Dad and her, it wasn't a hard record to break. The boys had known it was her birthday all along, they just wanted to make her think they'd forgot. Rude. She told them so. They were all appropriately apologetic and teasing at the same time. They'd all chipped in and got her a purple sleeping bag. Luca was pushing for a slumber party at his house during the break. His family apparently had a huge living room and people came over for slumber parties all the time. Honey wasn't sure she wanted to face his mom again anytime soon.

Lynn didn't just shower her with presents – she monsooned. She laughed when Honey told her that and offered to take back anything Honey didn't like or didn't think she would wear. It was all so nice, Honey couldn't decide what to send back and ended up keeping everything. Brayton got her a notebook and a package of pens. She suspected it was only because his mother told him to.

Zavier sent her a stuffed wolf from Yellowstone. Walter informed her in secret that he still hadn't been accepted into the pack, but his job was going well. Zavier would have sent a T-shirt, Walter said, but he didn't want to give anyone any clues to his whereabouts.

She was helping Lynn clean up when Brayton came by and stuck a small box in Honey's face.

"From Damien."

Luna Lynn looked up from the empty gift boxes she was collecting to reuse. "Why is Damien giving Honey a gift and why are you the delivery boy?" She looked around. "Where is he?"

"He was in the bathroom. He said it was an apology."

Brayton's face looked oddly blank and his voice was emotionless.

Honey didn't have to sniff very hard to smell the reason why.

"Thank you, Brayton. Can you set it on the table there? My hands are full," she lifted up a huge ball of wrapping paper that she'd rapidly grabbed.

"He said to give it to you."

"Setting it on the table is giving it to me. Please Brayton?"

To her relief, he listened. Luna Lynn dropped her pile of boxes into the large empty box she'd found somewhere and reached for Damien's gift.

"Don't touch it!" Honey warned.

Lynn didn't pull back, but she did stop the forward motion of her hand. "Why not?"

"It's spelled."

"That b… used a spell on me?" Brayton cursed.

"Brayton! Language! You know better than that."

"Sorry Mom. What kind of spell, Honey?"

She could smell the iron of shackles and the leather of the leash but no blood like she had with Brayton's curse and it wasn't nearly as strong.

"Compulsion I think."

Lynn pulled her hand back. "This is absolutely unacceptable. I'll have Alpha Brandon pay a visit to Alpha Meyer. Brayton, use a piece of wrapping paper and put that thing in this small gift bag. We'll need it for evidence."

"What will happen to him?" Honey asked.

"Probably nothing. The alphas generally take care of things like this and since he's the alpha's son…" Lynn let out a sigh. "On the other hand, Alpha Meyer is a proud man and he doesn't like people to see his underwear on the line. Since Damien attempted to use magic on another wolf not in his own pack, we also have the option to get the Coalition involved. I doubt Brandon will go that far, but he might report it so it's on record in case it happens again. I'll see if Chloe is available to guard you during finals next week, just to be safe."

Honey wanted to protest. She wasn't afraid of Damien, but at the same time, she didn't want to have to worry about him popping up when she needed to be focusing on exams.

"Thank you."

It was nice to see Chloe again. Horatio had proposed. Chloe said she was still thinking about it, but Honey was pretty sure of her answer.

Finals started. Damien didn't reappear. Honey heard from her friend Zuri in the Wolfborne pack who heard it from her uncle whose brother-in-law worked as a security guard at the pack house that Alpha Meyer had been furious with Damien. Things had been thrown and a window broken. Damien was relegated to the clean-up crew at the pack brewery.

It wasn't the same brewery that made Blue Wolf. Beer-making was apparently a popular business for wolves.

After her last exam on the last day of finals week, two hours before Brayton wanted to leave for the pack lands, she went to the library. She told Chloe that she had a very shy friend who wouldn't talk to her unless she was alone and she wanted to give her a gift. Chloe got all excited. She started giving Honey stranger danger warnings and telling her how she should never go off alone with someone unknown. Honey only convinced Chloe to leave her alone on the top floor of the library after Chloe did a complete search of the floor and found no one. Honey was sure that afterward, Chloe planted herself one floor below where she could watch the stairs and elevator.

Once Chloe was gone, Honey formed her shield and went through the janitor's door. It was probably hopeless, but she wanted to ask the librarian one last time to let her check out a history book. Also, Honey didn't know if the librarian had a family, but she seemed lonely and she had been helpful, albeit reluctantly. It only seemed right to make her a gingerbread cookie Christmas gift too.

When the librarian didn't immediately appear, Honey started exploring. That was a sure way to get the librarian's attention. Sure enough, a minute after Honey walked into the section where every book title contained the word 'charm' the librarian came silently tearing up the stairs. There was too much magic in the air for Honey to smell the spell, but only magic could explain how the librarian could be that quiet on metal stairs. A spell would also explain how the woman always managed to sneak up on her. Not this time though. Honey was waiting for her.

"Hello."

"You!" the librarian huffed.

"My name is Honey." The librarian knew that. She'd seen it on the letters Honey's friends had written.

"What are you looking for this time?"

"You. I figured if I started looking around you'd show up." Honey held out the baggie with her cookie. "I made you a present."

The librarian's nostrils flared while she inspected it. Frosting things was not one of Honey's better skills, so she fully understood the woman's skepticism. "It's a gingerbread man with an ugly sweater."

"I see."

"The colors weren't supposed to run together like that. It tastes good even if it looks strange."

The librarian lifted her face to study Honey's. "Why are you giving me this?"

"I made all my friends and teachers one."

"Which one am I?"

"You are an enigma."

The librarian snorted. "Thank you. I like that. I still can't let you check out any books."

"I know. Have a good Christmas. I have to go pack."

The librarian shook the bag. "Poisoning me won't get you what you want."

"I didn't poison it. You don't have to eat it. I just thought you'd like a present."

Honey turned to go. After living with both witches and wolves the last few months, the librarian's suspicion didn't surprise her at all, and it *was* one of the stranger-looking cookies she had made.

Behind her, the librarian let out a loud sigh. "Wait. Come with me. I can't let you borrow any books from the library, but I can let you borrow some from my private collection."

"Really?"

"One. We'll see how it goes. I know your name. I'll be able to find you if you don't return it."

"You only know my first name," Honey pointed out as they started back down the stairs.

"It's enough," the woman said mysteriously.

31

Honey

The pack house looked completely different than the last time Honey had visited. There were garlands and Christmas trees in every room, even Honey's bedroom, although the biggest by far was the one in the big open living room on the first floor. It was so tall it scraped the vaulted ceiling. The few days between the end of finals and Christmas were packed with preparations and gift wrapping. It was exhausting. Lynn never stopped and she seemed so excited to give Honey a 'real Christmas', that Honey felt obligated to help and do whatever Lynn asked. Brayton showed up for breakfast and dinner, but otherwise, he vanished.

Christmas Eve, at 5:30 pm, the preparation stopped. Luna Lynn hustled both her immediate family and the rest of the pack out to their cars dressed in their Christmas best to go to Christmas Eve services. Honey had never been to Lynn's denomination of church before. There was a lot of singing and a loud, boisterous pastor. Honey had trouble concentrating enough to pray.

Lynn came out of church nearly vibrating with excitement. "Are you ready to start partying? It's my favorite night of the year. You're going to love this. We're going to have hot apple cider and cocoa and popcorn and watch Christmas movies, and maybe open a gift or two."

Just down the street, the bells at the church of the denomination Honey normally attended started ringing. After all the busyness of the last week, kneeling in a quiet pew for a few moments was all she wanted to do.

"Do you mind if I go to my church first? It's just down the street."

"But we just went to church."

Honey looked down the street. It had been sprinkling all day. The colorful reflection of the church lights shining through the stain glass windows onto the wet pavement reminded her of a Thomas Kincaid puzzle she and her mom had bought from a garage sale. "I know but...."

"I'll take her, Mom," Brayton volunteered.

Lynn looked as surprised as Honey was. "You sure, Brayton?"

"Yeah." He turned to Honey. "You want to walk or have Dad drop us off?"

"How are you going to get home?" Lynn asked.

"I'll have Rhys pick us up."

Going to church with Brayton and only Brayton was going to be weird but if she didn't get away from everyone for a while, Honey was sure she was going to explode.

"Let's walk."

Brayton didn't say a word while they walked down the sidewalk. Despite his presence, she could feel herself relaxing the further they left the noise and the bustle around the first church behind. Half-way to their destination, she finally thought to thank him.

"I figured you needed a break," he replied. "I know you aren't used to a pack Christmas and Mom, well, she goes a little crazy this time of year. I'm guessing it was just you and your mom at Christmas?"

"Yeah, but we didn't stay home all day. Sometimes we'd go to a nearby retirement home or a hospital and visit with people. My mom..." Honey almost told him how her mom used her powers to heal people if she could, or just give them a better day if she couldn't. "My mom could make friends with anyone."

"Kind of like you."

"I guess."

Did Brayton just give her a complement?

"You okay?" he asked.

"Yeah."

"You're going to have to help me out. I've never been to this church before and I hear they do a lot of standing and sitting."

"And kneeling," she added. "Just do what I do."

There were a few rowdy children, and the pews were more crowded than usual, but the familiar environment felt peaceful. Thinking of Mary taking care of baby Jesus made her think of her mom and she started tearing up during the Gospel reading. Brayton, to her surprise, whipped out a little box of tissues, then leaned over and whispered 'Merry Christmas' in her ear, turning her sniff into a snicker. He held her hand during the Lord's prayer and hugged her when all the families around them started hugging as a sign of peace. Instead of being weird, it felt comfortable, almost like he was one of the guys. Almost.

It was still Brayton.

The day after a Christmas so filled with gift-giving and games and visiting that she just wanted to stay in bed the next day, Alpha Brandon called her into his office. He gave her a kind smile and nodded to the chair in front of his desk.

"Take a seat."

"Is something wrong?" she asked.

"No. I've got some news I thought you'd like to hear. Congratulations on your first semester grades, by the way. All A's. Very impressive considering everything that happened."

"Thank you."

She sat. For a wooden chair it was remarkably comfortable. Lynn must have picked it out.

He let out a long breath. "I guess there's no easier way to say this than to just let it out. We found your dad's motorcycle. It was in an impound lot. A motorist found it in a large ditch by the side of the road a couple of miles from where your house was. The tags and the VIN had been removed. I told Alpha Silver we discovered it in our attempt to find your mom's car. She had one, right?"

"Yes, but how did you know the motorcycle was my dad's if the tags and VIN were removed?" she asked.

"They didn't destroy the pack emblem on the gas tank."

"Emblem?"

"The little medallion with a picture of a red river."

She knew exactly what he was talking about. She'd seen it every time her dad let her sit on his bike or help him work on it. Dad loved his motorcycle. He rode it

247

everywhere, even in the freezing cold. Mom chastised him for that, then bought him magical gloves and jackets spelled to keep him warm no matter how fast he drove. Knowing the bike was gone too was like having another family member taken away.

"Here."

She took a tissue from the box Alpha Brandon was offering. She hadn't even noticed him moving around the desk.

It took a few minutes, but she finally composed herself. Dad was gone. She knew that. Alpha Brandon, meanwhile, was squatting next to her, rubbing her back. She wiped her face with yet another tissue and straightened. "Thank you for letting me know. Sorry I used up all your tissues."

"Don't worry, you didn't," he said as he stood. "Lynn keeps me well stocked. She seems to think a lot of crying goes on in here."

"Or she likes to shop."

"It could be that," he admitted with a wry grin while he sat back down at the desk. He looked down and cleared his throat. When he looked back up, his face was all serious again.

"There's more," she stated.

"Yes. Alpha Silver started an investigation of his own. He's going to discover the unidentified bodies in the house fire. They were too burned to identify by DNA and there's no reason he should associate the bodies or the fire with you, but I wanted you to be aware."

"Did you find my mom's car?"

"It was in the garage when the house burned down, but I'm not going to tell him that."

248

She shut her eyes against the tears threatening to flow again. "I'm glad you told him about the motorcycle. He should know."

"I agree. We need to figure out who killed them. If we can show it wasn't anyone from the Red River pack, then you can tell him who you are. I think the Silvers will be very happy to discover they have another family member. We need to figure out where your mom came from. Honey, do you remember anything like the emblem on the motorcycle that could tie your mom to a pack or anything your mom said that might give you a clue of where she came from? Did she tell you where she was born?"

He was trying so hard. She had to give him something or it would be suspicious. "A small town in Illinois somewhere. She never told me the name."

"She was from out of state?"

"Yes."

"How did your parents meet?"

"I don't know." True. She knew they met at college but she didn't know any specifics like where they were or if they ran into each other or someone introduced them. She wished she did.

"What about her family? Did she ever mention anything?"

"Not really."

"Nothing at all? Nothing like, 'this was my mom's favorite recipe' or 'Aunt Sally told horrible jokes?'"

"No. Sometimes she'd start to say something about her mom, then she'd press her lips together and smile and change the subject."

"Any letters or pictures or books?"

There was her mom's book of spells and recipes, but she wasn't about to mention that. "She didn't keep pictures of me and dad out in case someone broke in."

"Did she have a safe deposit box or some place she hid things?"

She did, but Honey wasn't supposed to tell anyone, and it had undoubtedly burned in the fire. "My dad has a shed," she blurted. One he'd told her to visit if he ever died, but she'd been putting it off.

"A shed?"

"For our dirt bikes."

"You have a dirt bike?"

"Yeah."

"Do you know where this shed is?"

She nodded.

He grinned, which made him look like Brayton's older brother instead of his dad. "I know where there's a track."

32

Brayton

"Turn here."

Brayton slammed on the brakes. "Here?" There wasn't a road. It didn't even look like there was enough room between the thick growth of young saplings to drive a vehicle. The only clue there was something there was a beat-up looking mailbox hidden in the tall, dead grass.

"Yes, see the tracks."

He turned onto the two ruts in the grass. His dad followed them in his truck. If they had to back out it would be challenging.

They drove for what must have been at least a quarter mile through the brush. It didn't feel right. They were probably trespassing on government property or something.

"Are you sure this is right?" He asked for the third time. Honey could be so stubborn. She probably didn't want to admit she was lost.

"Yes. We're here."

The trees abruptly gave way to a large clearing. There was a long, low building with a metal roof and a stove pipe that might be a house, a decent-sized wooden barn with a corrugated metal roof, and various smaller sheds. An old, beat-up truck from the 1970s was parked in front of the house.

"Park by that shed." She pointed to a wooden structure on the side of the barn that looked like it was about to collapse.

"Does someone live here? Should we introduce ourselves?" In his head he could hear banjos and see guys with overalls and shotguns.

"Charlie's coming."

The guy in the overalls with the shotgun wasn't just in Brayton's head. He was stomping across the packed-dirt driveway with a scowl on his scarred face that could frighten an alpha, or a future alpha. Honey opened the door and slipped out before Brayton could stop her and started waving at the man with a big, friendly grin.

"Hi Charlie. It's me."

It didn't stop the scowl. All it did was focus the man's attention on her.

"Honey," the man grunted. He stopped a few feet in front of her, his shotgun cradled in his arm, but at least not pointed at her. "Who are these guys? Where's your dad?"

Her voice was so soft Brayton could barely hear her. "He's gone Charlie."

"Gone? Gone where?"

Honey didn't say anything, just lifted a finger and pointed to the sky.

"Aw, girlie." Charlie pulled her into a brief one-armed hug. "He was a good man. What happened?"

"Fire." She stepped back and swiped at her face, then turned and waved to Brayton to come. "These are my friends. We're going riding."

Charlie eyed Brayton and his dad and his beta suspiciously when they lined up in front of him. "They look like a bunch of goons. Are they here to collect on a debt? Your dad wasn't that stupid."

Honey laughed, although it sounded forced. "No Charlie. They are nice people. This is Brandon Mooney and his friend and his son Brayton. They took me in after..."

"Your mom is gone too?" Charlie asked sharply.

"Yes."

"How?"

"House fire."

"You gonna be back?"

Honey shook her head. "I don't think so. It's not safe. I don't want whoever killed them to find you."

"You sure these guys are safe?"

"Well, they haven't killed me yet."

It was a lousy joke, or maybe Brayton was sensitive seeing as how he *had* nearly killed her.

Charlie jerked his head toward the shed. "Make sure you get everything then."

"Do I owe you any rent?"

"No. Your dad was all paid up." He abruptly turned and headed back to the house.

Honey didn't appear to notice Charlie's quick exit. She was focused on the shed. She undid the combination lock and disappeared into the dark. A moment later, a single bulb blinked to life in the center of the room.

Inside looked better than the outside, but only because of the neat way the bikes and gear were organized. The walls they were against were still leaning and the floor was dirt. There were also tools and spare parts lined up on a long, warped, wooden shelf.

"I see why you said we should bring two trucks," Dad said. "Is this your dad's bike?" He pointed to an all-black monster with silver detailing and a larger-than-normal engine.

"Yes." Honey laid her hand on the seat for several moments, then turned away. "I'll start boxing things up."

Brayton wanted to comfort her, but quickly talked himself out of it. He didn't want Dad getting any ideas about them, not until he was more certain about what he'd realized when he was looking for Honey in the library. He focused instead on getting her bike loaded into the truck he was driving.

Charlie reappeared after they were nearly through with a large envelope in hand. Honey smiled at him and quickly wiped her dirty hands on her jeans. "I've got something for you too."

"This isn't from me. It's from your dad." He held the envelope out to her. "It's a letter. He told me to give it to you if something ever happened to him."

Her smile fell and she reached for it. "Oh."

"I've got something else from him too. Follow me."

Brayton tailed along while Charlie led Honey to the big barn, not because he didn't trust him – okay, he didn't, but the man was human and he'd left his shotgun by the door of his house – but because he was curious. Charlie pushed

254

at the side of the large wooden door. The rollers in the rusty metal tracks above the door squealed in protest, but the door did move. Inside the barn, dust danced over a dirt-packed floor in the light shining through a single dirty window. Except for a workbench with a few tools along the far wall and a tarp-covered something in the center of the floor, the barn was empty. Charlie headed for the tarp.

"Your dad got a good deal on this a while back. He asked me to clean it up the last time I spoke with him, so I know he was planning on giving it to you this year." He waved his hand at the bike. "Go ahead, take a look."

Honey lifted the corner of the tarp and took a peek, then peeled it off completely, revealing a beautiful bike with a cobalt blue tank that looked like a cross between a motocross bike and a road bike.

"Is that street legal?" Brayton asked.

"Sure is," Charlie said.

Honey ran her hands over the handlebars. She had her back to him so Brayton couldn't see her face to tell what she was thinking.

"Wanna give her a spin? The tank's full," Charlie said.

"I…I can't." Honey dropped her head.

Brayton would have hugged her but Charlie beat him to it and put his arm over her shoulder. "Hey, girlie. Don't cry. Your dad wouldn't want you to cry over this. He was really looking forward to giving this to you. You know how he liked to give gifts. I'm sure he's watching you right now and wishing he could be here with you. Come on, this is a happy moment. He'd want you to be happy."

"I…I know. It's hard."

"Go on, go get your gear. Let's show your dad how she runs."

His mom was going to flip out. Brayton had mentioned getting a bike once back when he was in high school and his mom had harped about why he shouldn't get one until even he'd begun to question why they were allowed on the roads. He wondered if Honey's mom knew about the gift. Honey wasn't even sixteen. There was no way Dad would let her ride it.

Fifteen minutes later, they were on the highway with Honey on her bike behind them. It was only five miles to the track and the road was quiet, but it was still a highway. Dad hadn't even hesitated. He'd taken one look at Honey's tear-stained face and had asked her if she'd be warm enough.

Truthfully, Brayton didn't think he could have told her no either.

The track was understandably crowded. It was a clear day and everyone was eager to try out the Christmas gifts they couldn't try out the day before because of the weather. Brayton almost felt sorry for the disgruntled humans they passed when they pulled into the parking lot, but the track was pack owned and Dad only reserved it one day a year.

Honey parked a couple of spaces from the truck at the end of the row, sending bits of gravel flying. She took off her helmet and shook out her curls and it was just like one of those slow-motion scenes he'd seen in a couple of movies. He didn't realize he was staring until a group of high schoolers cut off his view. Gah, where was the handle? He finally got the door opened in time to hear one of the youngsters ask,

"Nice bike. Where did you get it?"

"It was a present."

"From your boyfriend?"

Could the boy be any more obvious?

"No."

"Luna Lynn?" This time the boy sounded rather shocked.

"No."

"Alpha Brandon?"

"My dad," Honey said softly.

"But your dad is…" Brayton could imagine the look Honey was giving the kid when he trailed off.

He was around the front of the truck by that time. "Hey guys. How's it going? How's Greenfield High?"

"Hey Brayton, it's great." One of the other boys said. "Not as great as when you were there though."

Brayton smiled instead of rolling his eyes. Did people think he couldn't tell when they were trying to suck-up or did they think he expected it?

"I'm sure it's exactly the same. Honey, come help me unload the bikes."

Too late, he realized he should have phrased it as a question, but she didn't protest. She meekly put her helmet down and walked around the boys and their bikes.

"Wow, who owns the black bike?" the third boy asked.

"It was my dad's," Honey answered.

"That's a nice bike. He must have been good."

"He was." Honey shared a smile with the boy. Brayton knew it didn't mean anything, but it was irritating that some random guy could make her smile so easily.

"Are you any good?"

"Guess you'll find out."

The kid saluted her with two fingers. "See you out there."

It was perfect. Not too pushy but enough to let her know he might be interested. By the way the first idiot elbowed him as they walked away, Brayton wasn't the only one to notice.

He removed the tie-downs and started unloading Honey's dirt bike.

"Just leave it, Brayton."

"Aren't you going to ride?"

She touched her chest where she must have stashed her dad's letter. "I want to be alone for a while."

How come every time there was a pack event, she found some way to miss it?

"I was hoping to see you ride."

"I'm sure there will be another time."

"Not soon. The whole pack only does this once a year. It's Dad's Christmas gift to the pack. I know you want to read your dad's letter, but we both know it will make you cry. You should wait until you're home in your room with a box of tissues."

"What are you trying to say, that I'm a cry-baby?"

"No, of course not." Why had he mentioned crying? "I just want to see you have a little fun. Come ride with me. The letter will still be here. You can put it in the glove compartment. I'll make sure to lock the doors. Come on, please?" With anyone else a 'for me' would have cinched it, but with Honey, that would probably have the exact opposite effect.

She bit her lip. He almost had her.

"Just a few times around. You might enjoy it, although probably not. You'll be eating my dust so…"

"There's no dust. It's all mud."

"It will be until I flame by."

258

"Flame. What, is your bike going to catch on fire?"

Her face fell. Shoot. Why had he mentioned flame? He jumped over the side of the bed and pulled her into a hug. "Sorry, Honey."

He could have sworn she relaxed against him for a moment before she pushed him away. "What are you doing?"

"You looked like you needed a hug."

She let out a loud sigh. "Fine, unload my bike."

Was that the secret to getting Honey to do what he wanted, give her random hugs? Maybe that's why she got along with Luca so well.

33

Honey

Darkness was falling when they left the track. Honey rode back in the truck. She hadn't practiced driving in the dark and she'd been riding all day anyway. Alpha Brandon found room for her new cycle in one of the trailers.

Lynn and several other women were waiting outside for everyone when they got back.

"Did everyone have fun? How many broken bones were there this year?" Lynn asked the moment Alpha Brandon opened his door.

Alpha Brandon stepped out of his truck and pulled Lynn into a hug, then kissed her cheek. "We did have fun and no one got hurt. See, you worry for nothing."

She pushed him away and waved her hand in front of her nose. "Ugh, you smell like gas and mud. Go take a shower."

"Brayton and Honey are dirtier than I am. I think they were trying to see which one of them could get muddier."

He wasn't wrong.

"You go ahead Alpha Brandon. I want to clean my bike while the mud is still wet." She looked around the circular drive where many of the pack buildings were clustered. "Where do you usually do that?"

"I'll show you," Brayton volunteered.

He'd been nice to her all day. If she didn't know better, she'd think he was as kind as her other friends.

"You found her bike then," Lynn asked.

"Yes. It was right where she said it would be. We found something else too."

Brayton jerked his head toward the truck, Honey followed him as slowly as she could. Alpha Brandon had said to let him tell Lynn about her gift, but she still wanted to hear what Lynn said.

"What?" Lynn asked behind Honey.

"Mike left Honey a birthday present and a letter."

"What did it say?"

"I don't know. She didn't share the contents with me. The gift is really nice though. You don't have to worry about finding her a car now."

Lynn looked around at all the trucks and SUVs and trailers filled with bikes and gear. "He got her a car? Where is it?"

"It's in one of the trailers."

It took Lynn a moment, then she said in a shocked voice, "He got her a bike! Was that man crazy? Did her mother know?"

"Yes, not that I know of, and I don't know. It's a good bike Lynn. It fits her well and she has a lot of experience. She was doing flips on her other one. She followed us to the track on it. She did well."

"You let her drive on the road? She doesn't even have a permit."

"There was hardly anyone on the road and she stayed behind us the whole way."

"No. Absolutely not. No fif…no teenage girl under my roof is going to drive a motorcycle. It's too dangerous."

"Lynn, like you said, she doesn't have a permit yet. She can't drive it now, and it's a gift from her dad. I don't think we have any right to tell her she can't ride it. He bought it for her years ago. You know Mike. He was crazy about bikes. He probably had her on one before she could walk."

"I don't like it."

He put his arm around her and started steering her toward their house. "I know."

"They're dangerous."

"Any time you get on the road it's dangerous. There are lots of people who've ridden bikes for years and never had an accident."

Lynn punched him lightly on the arm. "You always say that."

"And I'm always right."

Honey waited until they were out of hearing before she asked Brayton, "What does she have against bikes?"

"Her dad got into a serious accident when she was a teenager. He died."

"Oh."

"Yeah. That's why I drive an SUV."

Well past an hour later, Honey's bike was clean and stowed with the rest of the pack bikes. She was clean too, her belly was full, and she finally had time to herself. She sat down at the desk in her room and carefully pried open the yellow envelope from her dad. The page full of her dad's messy handwriting made her heart lurch painfully, but at the same time it was a page full of her dad's handwriting, something she didn't think she'd ever see again. She smoothed out the paper and began to read.

Dear Honey,

I love you. I've loved you from the first moment I saw you and I still love you even though I can't be with you anymore. You are my fated daughter and you will always be.

I know I've told you all that a hundred times before, but if you are reading this letter, then it's time I explain. First though, I want you to know that I've wanted to tell you this so many times. I didn't want to keep any more secrets from you than we already were, but your mother was afraid if someone caught you or you got lost you might accidentally let something slip. I know you wouldn't, not now that you're older, and if you've got this letter and not the other one, then both your mom and I are gone so most of it doesn't matter anymore except to you.

Okay, fated daughter, what does that mean? It means that I am not your biological father. It means that I wasn't aware of your existence until a couple of weeks before you were born. It means that the moment I held you in my arms, even though you were all slippery and purple-colored, I knew I was meant to be your dad.

I knew your mom before you were born. That's why she came to me for help. She and your biological father, my brother, were good friends in college, and only friends as far as I knew. Your mom told you about the feud between our families. A relationship between them was even more impossible than for anyone else because they were both slated to become leaders in their respective communities. On top of

263

that, your mom was engaged to someone else. It wasn't her choice. It was a marriage arranged by her family. Apparently, that still happens in her family even though they have lived in the US for generations.

I'm not sure exactly how, I mean I know HOW but not how they ended up...anyway a couple of months before graduation, your parents came together and boom! there you were. It still blows my mind when I think of it. At that time in their lives, both of them were strictly by the book. I can't even imagine them kissing let alone...you know what I mean. The only explanation I have is that fate (or God) had a hand in your creation, and that, I'm absolutely positive, is what happened.

Your mom knew that my brother was never going to be in a position where he could marry her. She couldn't go back to her own family carrying a child of the enemy and, as you are aware, they would have figured out the truth. She couldn't bring herself to terminate the pregnancy either. She decided to disappear for a while, just until she had you. I don't know if she explained to you why our two families don't ever get together. She was planning to once you were old enough. It's a sad story. Anyway, if the stories were true, she didn't expect that you would live, but she wanted to give you a chance.

She started by traveling around the country. She collected postcards, much more than she sent, to cover any months she wouldn't be able to travel. She was planning to have you by herself, you know what your mom was, but the closer the time came, the more she realized how hard that was going to be. She was afraid to go to anyone in her community. Her family has ways of making people talk, so she went to the one person who wasn't part of her community and knew about her friendship with your father yet hadn't told a soul — me.

264

I tried to talk her into finding a midwife or just popping into the normal hospital on the day of, but she was adamant that we keep everything secret. She was afraid that if the stories were true, the media would hear about you and that would be a disaster for everyone.

So for the next month, I read everything I could about childbirth. I studied harder for that day than any exam I've ever taken before or after. I made a kit and carried it around in my car. That's right, I said car. Don't judge. Finals were coming up. I was afraid your mom would call me in the middle of an exam, but you were very considerate and decided to come the Saturday before finals.

You know the rest. I was there when you were born. I was the first person to hold you and look into your beautiful eyes. All your mom's worrying was for naught except now she had another problem: what to do with you.

I offered to take you. I was only a Junior in college at the time and I didn't have a girlfriend so it would have been rather challenging to explain, but I was willing to try. Your mom said no. She would raise you by herself. I didn't need to concern myself with either of you anymore.

I put my foot down to that. I told her right then that it was too late, that I was in, and that you were my daughter.

She laughed. It took me two years to convince her otherwise, but eventually, she realized I meant it. I loved your mom. She was a wonderful, strong, brave, smart, and talented woman, but I loved you first. Every time I had to go away on a trip, I missed you. Every day I had to stay away, I missed you. That day in the park when you were six was one of the happiest in my life. I nearly called my brother to brag about my daughter. Can you imagine what a shock that would have been?

I'm not going to give you names. You're smart enough to figure it out. I think it will be safe to tell my brother who you are. I never did because he had enough going on and I didn't want to go against your mother's wishes, but she's gone and you're both older now. If you need someone, you should go to him. You know which school I went to. You can probably find my picture somewhere and get some clues.

Your mom's family is dangerous. I think it might be safe to talk to her mom, but definitely not her grandmother, at least from what your mom told me. If we're dead and you're not, I'd guess it was someone from her side, or at least from her community. On the other hand, there are some on my side, not the immediate family, that could have done it too.

If you need immediate funds, sell my dirt bike. My brother will likely keep the other one. If you need more cash than you can get from the bike, just remember what happened on June 15, and go there. I started a savings account (a Honey pot, get it?) when you were young. I left a clue. Even if you are reading this a century after I wrote it (wouldn't that be cool?) the clue will still be there, unless aliens invade and destroy the world as we know it, in which case, the bank probably won't be there anymore either. Only you should be able to see the clue or bother looking anyway.

I'll say it again. I love you. It was my immense pleasure to know you and care for you. You are something special. I leave it up to you whether to show this letter to my brother or not. He is a good man. The only danger is his position. All people who do what he does have to swear to uphold the law. He won't, not in your case, but if anyone found out about it, it would put his entire extended family in danger. If he were to meet you, that wouldn't matter to him, but I wanted to make sure you understood.

With all my love, forever,
Your fated Father.

Honey wiped her tears and blew her nose and read the letter again. Dad wasn't her dad? Mom had lied to her, her entire life? For once, she was too numb to cry. The wonderful, wonderful man who'd raised her wasn't her dad at all, just a younger brother taking care of his older brother's mess. And he'd done it despite what she was and despite how dangerous it was to associate with her. She wished with all her heart he was there and she could hug him one more time.

Wait, that meant Alpha Silver wasn't just her uncle. He was her biological father.

Notes from the Author

Want more of Honey's antics? You're in luck. Honey's got a big adventure ahead of her. It took me seven books to tell the whole story. They're already written and nearly ready to be published so if they aren't online yet, they should be shortly.

Reader feedback is very much appreciated. Please leave a review if you liked the story and tell your friends and your librarian. (That's me marketing. Impressive, right?)

You may have noticed the 'Clean Fiction' logo at the beginning of the book. I love to read but sometimes, okay often, find myself in the middle of a good story and abruptly I'm in someone's bedroom getting a play-by-play. Sex happens but I don't need to be there. I'm not the only one who feels this way. I discovered whole communities on Instagram and a magazine on Amazon devoted to clean reads. To make it easier for like-minded people to find clean books and to encourage other authors to go clean, I thought a logo on said books would be helpful. So, if you are a writer or know one and would like a copy of the logo, drop me a line. LisaL.author@gmail.com. I'd be glad to share. I have both gold-foil and black-ink versions.